'Cenna…' Phil's voice was rough and husky, trying to get a grip.

'I don't know if I should apologise or…' He lowered his head, though his hands still trapped her. Then he looked slowly up and she knew what he had been going to say. She willed him to say it, but he didn't. Instead he released her, his shoulders hunched under the blue cotton.

'Phil, I don't want you to apologise.' Her answer surprised her. From somewhere deep down she found the strength to tell the truth. 'I wanted you to kiss me.'

Join the

Country Partners

in these two fabulous linked titles by Carol Wood:

Meet the partners in this lively rural practice. In this bustling community, nestled in the heart of Dorset, the doctors of the Nair Surgery are kept busy with the trials of their patients, friends and colleagues.

But can they find time for their own lives, and loves? Will these country partners become partners—for life?

THE HONOURABLE DOCTOR
Discover whether Dr Marcus Granger
and Dr Jane Court can rekindle their love….

THE PATIENT DOCTOR
Will Cenna be able to convince the irresistible
Dr Phil Granger to love again?

Country Partners
Care in the community—love in the surgery.

THE PATIENT DOCTOR

BY

CAROL WOOD

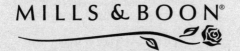

MILLS & BOON®

First published in Great Britain 2001
Harlequin Mills & Boon Limited,
Eton House, 18-24 Paradise Road, Richmond, Surrey TW9 1SR

© Carol Roma Wood 2001

ISBN 0 263 82693 7

Set in Times Roman 10½ on 11½ pt.
03-1001-50335

Printed and bound in Spain
by Litografia Rosés, S.A., Barcelona

CHAPTER ONE

CENNA gazed out of the window, a pang of guilt going through her at her shameless curiosity. The two figures, deep in conversation, stood under the trees of the surgery car park. One was Dr Phil Jardine, a tall, dark-haired, lean man and senior partner of Nair Surgery. The other was Dr Helen Prior from nearby Stockton Practice, dressed in a slim-fitting navy blue suit and high heels.

In her early forties, there was no question that Helen was still a beautiful woman. Cenna noticed that the female doctor had recently cut her long dark hair and now wore it short, tucked fashionably around her ears. Her visits to the surgery had increased since Phil's young wife had died the Christmas before last.

Cenna studied her partner's face but was too far away to see his expression. Only Helen Prior's easy laughter drifted back through the open window.

Finally turning away, Cenna returned to her desk and the hospital reports waiting for her inspection. She leafed through them slowly, her distracted expression hidden by her long, dark hair, highlighted by waves of chestnut as it fell gently across her face. Why shouldn't Phil be attracted to Helen Prior? she asked herself reasonably. It was, after all, fourteen months now since Maggie's death in a skiing accident. Time he picked up the threads of a new life...

Just then there was a knock at the door and Annie Sharpe, one of the afternoon receptionists, appeared. 'Your last two patients have arrived, Dr Lloyd. Mrs Gardiner, a new patient signed on this morning. And Louise Ryman.'

5

'Louise?' Cenna frowned. 'I saw her last month—in January, I think.'

Annie nodded. 'According to records, yes. Actually, I'm a bit worried about Louise…you know she teaches Callum, my thirteen-year-old? Well, she's so good with the kids, takes them all in her stride, but lately she's not looked well. I hope there's nothing wrong. Teaching can be very stressful. I know I couldn't cope with it.'

Cenna grinned ruefully as she glanced up under her dark lashes. 'You cope with a busy GP practice, Annie. I should have thought that was equally as stressful.'

'You're different.' Annie laughed as she looked at Cenna over the top of her half-moon reading spectacles. 'You're human. If my three tearaways are anything to go by, a class of teenagers would frighten the life out of me, going by what our Callum says. You know—'

Cenna held up her hand. 'Don't, Annie! No more horror stories today.'

The receptionist grinned mischievously. 'Oh, come on, now, Dr Lloyd. Surely you want to hear the story of the party from hell whilst the parents were away? Or what treasures can be found stuffed under the mattress when Mum decides to spring-clean?'

'No way, Annie!' Cenna protested just as the door opened again.

'Sounds interesting.' Phil Jardine, his dark brown eyebrows lifting, walked in the open door. 'Can anyone join in this conversation?' Dressed in a smart dark suit and unusually pristine white shirt, he caused the two women to chuckle as he cupped his hand to his ear. 'What was that you said about mattresses, Annie?'

'Oh, nothing you haven't heard before, Dr Jardine,' the plump, middle-aged receptionist said with a laugh. 'I expect you could write a book on all you've heard over the years.'

'Come on,' Phil said with sudden mock disappointment,

'I'm not Methuselah. I'll have you know I slave hours at the ironing-board, just trying to keep up with you girls.'

The two women burst into laughter and Annie screwed up her nose. 'Oh, Dr Jardine, you're just a spring chicken yet. Wait till you get to my age and then you can complain.'

Cenna listened to Phil talking with Annie and allowed herself the luxury of studying her partner's craggy features, unobserved. The shock of his wife's tragic death in a holiday accident had carved lines in his strong face and given everyone who knew him cause for concern. But he seemed to have won the battle with his grief and at thirty-nine was a ruggedly handsome man, though anyone not knowing his history might guess at the sadness hidden in his dark eyes.

Cenna allowed her gaze to linger on the pelt of thick, dark brown hair, newly cut and tamed, ending neatly at his collar. Was Phil really considering an affair with Helen? she wondered.

Annie left the room and Cenna realised Phil was grinning at her. He sat down on the chair beside her desk. 'Are you going to tell me what you've been daydreaming about for the last five minutes?' he teased.

She couldn't disguise a blush, dragging her concentration—and caution—back to the moment. 'Oh, just planning a holiday somewhere. A golden beach, blue skies, that sort of thing.'

'Anywhere special? Or should I say *with* anyone special?'

'Not really.' She shrugged. 'I might join a group from the gym going to Crete—a watersports holiday. We're having a meeting on Saturday to discuss it. No doubt it will be fun.'

Phil frowned, a smile hovering on his lips. 'Oh, that surprises me.'

'What surprises you?' she asked hesitantly. 'A watersports holiday?'

'No, not the holiday—just that you and Mark aren't planning a break together.'

'Mark?' She blinked. 'I've no idea where Mark's holidaying this year.'

Phil looked at her with a frown. 'I rather thought you two were…' He stopped and shrugged.

'Were what?' Cenna asked quickly.

'Oh, I don't know—an item, I suppose.' He gave her a twisted smile as she stared at him. 'Look, forget it. Sorry I asked.'

'Phil, I don't mind you asking, but I don't know why you should think—'

'Whoa,' he said firmly, shaking his dark head. 'It's OK. You don't want to talk about it and that's fine by me. I had no idea Mark Paget was such a sensitive subject.'

'He's not,' Cenna answered abruptly, the colour flooding to her face. 'It's just that I don't like to discuss my private life at—'

'Understood,' Phil said, cutting her short.

Cenna stared at him, wondering how their discussion had suddenly become so tense. Had it something to do with her relationship with Mark? 'I would have thought you of all people would have understood,' she said quickly. 'When it comes to discussing Maggie—well, you never do. At least, not here in a professional environment…' Her words petered out. She was getting in too deep.

His face darkened. 'Maggie is gone—and that's all there is to it, end of story,' he told her. 'There's nothing to discuss.'

'Isn't there?' Cenna asked slowly.

'No.'

'Look, Phil, I'm just making some sort of comparison. After Maggie's death, you seemed reluctant to discuss her and maybe that was your way of handling things, and—'

'And you're saying that your way of handling your relationship with Mark is entirely private and that I should mind my own business.'

She sighed. 'This has all got rather out of hand—'

'I agree,' he cut in with a sharp nod as he turned and walked to the door.

'Phil?' She didn't know why, but all too often they seemed to be treading on one another's toes. 'Please, don't take what I said personally. Put it down to one TR too many, will you?'

He met her eyes and gave her the briefest of smiles. 'We've all been a bit pushed lately.' He shrugged. 'No offence taken.'

The door closed and she let out a long sigh. Why had she been so sensitive about Mark? She felt nothing for Mark now, even though they had once been close. And why was Phil so defensive about Maggie?

Maggie Jardine... As Cenna thought of her now she recalled the tall, reed-slender woman of twenty-seven who had been Phil's wife. Like Helen Prior, Maggie had been exceptionally lovely.

Surely she couldn't be feeling jealous of Helen...could she? And if she was, why? There was no involvement between her and Phil...at least, she didn't think so. In fact, the short while they had spent alone together at that party last year had made it clear to her that she was determined to avoid any involvement. Mark had hurt her deeply. And the pain had lasted a long, long time...

What, she wondered, had made Phil ask about Mark Paget?

When the internal phone rang again, it was Annie to say that Louise Ryman was waiting. Trying to put the recent events out of mind, Cenna smiled at the attractive young redhead who entered the room.

'I'm tired all the time,' Louise complained wearily, a twenty-six-year-old technology teacher. 'It isn't like me at all. I enjoy IT and think it's vital for the kids to learn with computers. But lately I just feel stressed out at the job.'

'How's your appetite?' Cenna thought that her patient looked rather thin and had definitely lost weight since the last time she had seen her.

Louise paused. 'Cooking for one isn't really appealing.' She bit her lip and added, 'My partner has just moved out and…and I've found it quite difficult adjusting.'

'I'm sorry to hear that,' Cenna commiserated. 'But you should try to eat a balanced diet. I'm sure you know how important that is.'

Louise nodded. 'Yes, I'm always telling the kids not to stuff themselves with junk food.'

After talking to Louise for a little longer and taking a blood sample, Cenna asked her patient to make a follow-up appointment. It was, she felt, highly likely that Louise was anaemic. However, this could only be confirmed when the test results came through.

Her next patient, Mary Gardiner, was a tall, elegant brunette in her early thirties who had just moved to Nair with her husband. 'I keep in good health,' she explained, 'but I do suffer from migraine and take medication for it when I have an attack.'

Cenna did not have any previous records to refer to but assured her new patient that she would prescribe the requested drug should an attack begin.

'We've taken over a hotel in the town centre—the Summerville,' Mary Gardiner went on to tell her. 'Ray is a chef and he specialises in French cooking, so we're hoping to build the business up.' She delved into her bag. 'Here are two complimentary invitations to eat in the restaurant, either this Saturday or the next. Bring a friend and one of the meals will be on the house. We promise not to disappoint.' She smiled as she got up to leave.

'The food's good apparently,' Annie told her later. 'According to the reviews in the *Evening Echo*.'

'Maybe I'll go.' Cenna shrugged. 'She seemed a very pleasant person.'

'Well, you'll never know till you try.' Annie grinned before leaving. 'You did say she'd given you two invitations?'

Cenna glanced wryly at the departing figure. 'Yes. One meal is free—quite a tempting offer. Do you fancy coming, Annie?'

Annie stopped at the door. 'To be honest, I'm not really into French food. Traditional English cuisine, that's me. But how about asking Dr Jardine? You'd be the first to agree he needs to relax more.'

Flushing slightly under Annie's scrutiny, Cenna smiled. 'Relax, yes—talk shop, no. And the chances are we'd probably end up doing that. You know what it is when doctors get together.'

Annie gave her an odd glance, then sighed softly. 'Well, someone else will make the offer, I expect.'

Trying to decipher what Annie meant by this, Cenna wondered if she really did have the courage to ask Phil out to dinner. After their altercation the other day, it might be a way back to resuming normality. Since Maggie's death, he seemed to have erected an invisible shield around himself, fielding anything personal with his wry sense of humour—which, she had to admit, usually worked.

To be fair, she really had tried hard to get through to him on a professional level and she had succeeded. They worked well together. But after the incident at the staff party last year, the distance between them seemed to have widened.

Cenna's mind drifted back to the occasion. It had been a party given at her own house in celebration of the new surgery. The party had gone on until just before midnight and only Phil had remained. He had accepted her offer of a hot drink before leaving and it had been evident they'd still been on a high, knowing the evening had been a success. Planning permission for the extension of the new practice had been complete. Phil's dream had finally come true. They had been on their way. The night had seemed very special.

In the quietness, Phil had turned to her, his arm brushing briefly against hers. His eyes had met hers and the silence had deepened as some strange energy had passed between them. She had thought about it many times since, wondering what would have happened had the phone not rung. Someone had forgotten their coat and she'd promised to take it in to the surgery the following day. By the time she'd come off the phone, Phil had been shrugging on his jacket, ready to leave.

Cenna sighed and, turning to her computer, flashed up the details of her next patient, Homer Pomeroy. He was a sixty-two-year-old man with a history of gout. Gaynor Botterill, the practice nurse, had referred him to Cenna after his latest BP check.

Silver-haired, smartly dressed in a faultless grey suit and well spoken, Homer announced he was marrying for the third time and had every intention of celebrating the fact.

'When is the wedding?' Cenna asked as she smelt a potent mixture of alcohol and cologne flow over her desk.

'Haven't set the date yet, my dear, but not long, not long. Can't keep my beautiful bride waiting—she might change her mind,' Homer joked.

After knowing Homer for several years, she was aware of her patient's appetite for the finer things of life. A wealthy man, with all the trappings of a successful career in the City, he made no bones about his determination to savour his retirement.

'I'm sure you're both eager to get on with the wedding,' Cenna commented, 'but until then, I would advise caution.'

'Absolutely,' Homer agreed effusively. 'Now, all I want you to do, my dear, is give this knee of mine a bit of a tweak.'

Cenna knew he was referring to a corticosteroid drug for pain relief which she had previously injected into his swollen knee. However, she was reluctant to do this until she was given some assurance that Homer was helping himself.

'Have you your medication with you?' she asked, knowing that almost certainly he did not. He had once complained bitterly that his anti-inflammatory drugs spoilt the taste of his cocktails.

'Can't abide pills, m'dear. Prefer the needle, you know. Short and sharp, gets the job done.'

'If the level of uric acid in your blood is high again, Mr Pomeroy,' Cenna warned firmly, 'drug treatment for your gout will need to be continued permanently to prevent hypertension.'

The older man looked horrified. 'But, my dear, this is just a touch of arthritis!'

'Well, we've discussed this before,' Cenna said with a sigh, recalling the times they'd had this conversation. 'I won't argue with you, but I'll aspirate some of the fluid in your knee and send it for analysis. Then we'll have a chat again when we get the results.'

'Eminently sensible, young woman. But for now—'

'For now, I'll have a look at your leg and decide what to do,' Cenna conceded.

A compromise struck, Cenna nevertheless found herself administering the corticosteroid drug with an assurance from Homer that he would change his ways and return to see her the following month.

Cenna wondered if his bride-to-be was aware of the full facts of her future husband's ill health. But as she glanced out of the window at Homer's large and expensive car outside and the lovely young woman sitting at the wheel, she guessed not.

It was a typically busy Friday afternoon. The antenatal clinic was finished and mothers and small children were filing out from the new extension that comprised specially equipped treatment rooms.

The light and airy corridors of Nair Surgery were slowly emptying and Cenna was walking towards Reception when Phil came out of one of the doors on the right. He held the door open for a last mum-to-be to exit with her toddler.

'That's it for today,' he sighed as he peeled the stethoscope from around his neck. He glanced at his watch, his dark brown eyes coming up to meet Cenna's. 'How about you?'

'I've a late surgery this evening,' she told him as she saw her next patient approaching. 'And I think we've one or two emergency appointments.'

'Anything I can do to help?' he offered as they began to walk together down the corridor.

'I don't think so, but thanks,' she answered a little stiltedly. He was trying to be friendly and after Monday's episode she wanted to get back on track. She had thought about things a lot over the last few days. Whatever odd feelings she'd had about Phil and Helen that morning, well, they had just been passing. A figment of her imagination—something as spurious as that. She would like to know there were no hard feelings between them, and if she didn't ask him now she never would.

'Phil…?' She bit her lip, pushing back her dark hair hesitantly. 'One of my patients has recently moved to Nair with her husband and they've bought a hotel—'

'You don't mean the Summerville, by any chance?' Phil interrupted as they stopped outside his room.

'Yes, that's right,' she answered in surprise.

'And you have two complimentary tickets to eat there?'

'How did you know?'

'Ray Gardiner signed on with me yesterday. The good man also left two with me. I must say that's a pretty good marketing exercise,' Phil arched a dark eyebrow. 'However, I'm busy tomorrow night so I've decided to give them to Marcus and Jane. I know they've been busy decorating lately and thought they might like the opportunity of a night out. If they do go they'll be able to tell you firsthand what the grub's like.'

She managed a smile. 'Oh, thanks.'

'Cenna?'

She looked up at him.

'About the other day—our disagreement—it's forgotten?'

She gave him a bright smile. 'Of course.'

He looked at her for a few minutes before giving her that twisted grin of his. 'OK, well, that's fine, then.'

Feeling a fool, she watched him walk away. Had he guessed what she'd been about to ask him and fielded her question? She had even planned what she was going to wear. And even more stupidly had imagined that Phil would have nothing better to do with his Saturday evening than spend it with her.

Dr Jane Granger felt her baby kick and for a moment she paused, imagining the tiny hands and feet turning inside. She had only one concern and that was her blood pressure. It was a little too high. She hadn't told Marcus, of course. He would insist she stop work immediately.

With good intentions in mind, eating a healthier, less rushed diet and resting at home, she would soon have things back under control.

Her morning surgery over, Jane lifted the small pile of

prescriptions she had signed, ready for collection on Monday, and made her way out to Reception. The newly carpeted corridor with its thick grey-blue weave seemed very luxurious. She couldn't help but feel slightly awed at the sophistication of Nair Surgery. Over three months after the opening—and she still wasn't accustomed to it.

The wide reception spaces and modern seating, a children's crèche area and individual rooms for complementary treatments—all decorated in tasteful pastel colours and an abundance of natural light from the wide windows. Phil had at last achieved the goal he had planned towards for so long. Dr Jardine, senior, would have been proud of his son.

Jane opened the door to her right, entering the office behind Reception. She was surprised to find Phil and Helen Prior there.

'Oh, I didn't expect to see you here today, Phil,' Jane said quickly as she lowered the prescriptions to the table.

'I'm on call,' Phil told her. 'Just popped in for some paperwork.'

'Hello, Jane,' Helen said. 'I'm, er…just returning a medical journal Phil lent me.' There was a rather awkward silence before Helen added, 'How are you feeling?'

'Ravenous, actually.' Jane patted the bulge under her skirt. 'I've a morning craving for hot crusty bread and pickles of all things. Oh, and talking of food, that reminds me. I'm sorry, Phil, but Marcus and I won't be able to use the Summerville tickets this evening.'

'Oh, that's a pity,' Phil said with a frown.

'It's Ben's birthday, you see,' Jane added as she took the two tickets from her bag and handed them over. 'Darren's staying for the night.'

'Shame.' Phil shrugged his broad shoulders as he took them. 'The French food offer did sound rather exciting.'

'French food? I love it,' said Helen Prior quickly. The attractive, dark-haired doctor glanced at Phil.

'Well, I had these two tickets…' Phil began. Looking rather flustered, he went on hesitantly, 'An introductory offer, which it seemed a shame to waste…'

'I'd love to go,' Helen said quickly. 'That is if you are, Phil.'

'Well, I did have a prior arrangement,' Phil murmured, looking awkwardly at Jane.

Again, there was a pause. Jane noticed that Helen's dark eyes were fixed on Phil, her expression expectant.

'Well, I must go,' Jane said quickly. 'I'm collecting Darren on my way home. Goodbye, Helen.'

'Nice to see you again, Jane.' Helen's gaze was still on Phil and the tickets in his hand.

'Bye, Jane,' Phil called.

Jane couldn't help but glance back as she closed the door. She hated to think she was curious—but she was. Phil and Helen Prior of all people. Surely not? Her last glimpse was of Helen looking up at Phil. She was obviously attracted to him. But was Phil attracted to her?

Somehow Helen didn't seem Phil's type at all…but, then, neither had Maggie. Phil had met Maggie whilst abroad on holiday. Maggie, then a model, had been on a photo shoot for a magazine. Phil had reversed his hired car into some of the photographer's equipment. Everyone had been stunned at their whirlwind romance and marriage three months later.

Jane retraced her steps to her room to turn off her computer before leaving. The building seemed very quiet as she sat at her desk for a few moments, giving thought to the odd event that had just taken place. Had she misinterpreted the situation? Would Phil take Helen Prior to the Summerville?

Leaving the surgery by the back door and stepping out into the fresh air, Jane tried to assemble her thoughts for home. She was going to collect Darren on the drive back to the house. Marcus had suggested they eat out and Ben had been excited all week. But as much as she tried to concentrate on the afternoon before her, she was disturbed by what she had seen at the practice.

Was there really a romantic link between the female GP and Phil?

CHAPTER TWO

CENNA replaced the phone and sighed. Now she wouldn't get the room finished tonight. The rest of the decorating would have to wait until tomorrow. Why, she asked herself, had she agreed to Mark's suggestion?

Because he's going, a little voice inside her whispered. And she was relieved.

'I don't want our relationship to end on a bitter note,' he had told her in that smooth, dripping-with-charm voice that now made her cringe.

'I hold no hard feelings,' Cenna had assured him.

'I hope not, Cenna. Actually, I've some news for you. I've decided to accept a job abroad—with a rather well-known firm of lawyers.'

She smiled to herself. Mark must have loved telling her that. 'I'd like to say goodbye as friends,' he had continued. 'After all, we have known each other since we were kids.'

It was probably that, she realised, that had prompted her to agree. They did go a long way back. She hadn't forgotten the pain he'd caused her, but she had forgiven him. Since moving south, her life had changed. For the better.

Underneath a wing of glossy brown hair, Cenna's large amber eyes were distracted as her thoughts went back to the past. She'd had to make some difficult choices before moving to Nair. Her roots were in the Midlands. But breaking up with Mark during her training year had settled the question of her future.

As the only child of older parents who had both passed away, there had seemed nothing to anchor her to the small town in which she had grown up. And when she had answered Phil's advertisement in a medical journal, and Phil had asked her to join the practice in Dorset, her decision had been made without hesitation.

Mark had phoned her last Christmas, explaining his mother had relations to visit in Southampton. Ellen Paget was Cenna's mother's oldest friend and Cenna had felt unable to refuse when Mark had suggested a meeting.

After Mrs Paget's brief but pleasant visit, Mark had called several times at the practice. Cenna had been polite, introducing him as an old friend, but when he had turned up at the house unannounced one day, they had quarrelled.

Today he had phoned and apologised. It had been with deep relief that Cenna had heard his news. And saying that the meal was at her expense made her feel better. She didn't want to be in Mark's debt and he knew it.

'Bother,' she sighed to herself, pushing the paintbrush she was holding a little too forcefully into a pot of turps. It spilled and she wiped it with a rag, wishing that, America or not, Mark Paget hadn't just upset her plans for the evening.

Dressed in jeans and a lime green baggy jumper with her hair tied back in scarf, Cenna realised the half-finished project of her dining room would have to wait. Her suggestion that they eat at the Summerville meant she'd have to find something decent to wear!

Her carriage clock in the bedroom said eight fifteen. Cenna glanced one last time at her reflection in the mirror.

The floaty pale blue dress looked summery, yet not too sophisticated. Its simple lines allowed her to wear her favourite strappy white high heels which would have made an evening dress look over-fussy.

She twirled once, the soft blue chiffon moulding itself sleekly around her body, perhaps making her look a little taller than her five-seven. She had planned to wear this dress with Phil and now the presumption of such a thought made her blush.

What had made her think Phil would accept? And even if he had, this would almost certainly have been because he wouldn't have wanted to hurt her feelings. If only she had stopped to think, she might have realised that asking him point-blank would have put him in an impossible position. As it was, he had managed to save them both embarrassment…

Now, why had she thought of Phil? she wondered as she gazed at her reflection, her amber eyes partially hidden under the dark waterfall of freshly washed hair that fell around her shoulders.

Silly, but the thought of her partner caused a stab of excitement inside her. She had been trying to work up some enthusiasm for the evening ahead, unsuccessfully. A few final adjustments to make, a little lip-gloss, a very, very small amount of blusher—with her tawny skin, she needed only a hint dusted on her cheeks. And the palest of eye-shadow—a soft cinnamon enhancing the golden flecks of her amber eyes under her dark eyelashes. She wished suddenly that it was Phil she was seeing. She almost laughed. A ridiculous and impractical notion…

Mark was already in the bar when she arrived. Cenna had driven herself, intending to leave as soon as the meal was over. Mark beckoned to her, his admiring blue eyes telling her that he approved of what she had chosen to wear. There was no doubt that he cut a handsome figure in a fashionable dark suit and tie, his blond hair smoothed back from his tanned face, and for an uncomfortable moment she recalled the way he had always enjoyed female attention.

More painful memories followed as Cenna walked towards him, recalling how upset she had been at the discovery of his affair. It had happened during her training at a

Midlands hospital, and possibly because they had known each other for so many years, his betrayal had come as a stomach-churning shock.

'You look wonderful,' Mark told her in that voice that brought her sharply back to reality. He ordered the soft drink she asked for and, taking the stool beside her, began his usual easy flow of conversation.

A few minutes later Mary joined them. 'It's so nice to see you,' she told Cenna. Glancing at them both, she asked, 'Your table is booked for eight, but would you like to see the rest of the hotel first?'

'Yes, I would,' Cenna answered, but Mark shook his head.

'I'll wait,' he said rather sharply.

Grateful for the opportunity to be away from Mark, Cenna enjoyed the tour, recalling how she'd visited the hotel once before some years ago. The Gardiners had transformed the rooms with fresh designs and had completely refurbished the kitchen. Ray Gardiner had time to pass only a few words with her as he worked skilfully over the sparkling new equipment.

Afterwards, Mary showed them both to a table in the restaurant. The deep red tablecloths and tall glassware added a continental flavour to the atmosphere and the consommé smelt delicious.

'Are you enjoying your meal?' Mary asked as she removed their dishes a little later.

'Yes, very much,' Cenna replied. 'Please, tell Ray the consommé was delicious.'

'He'll be pleased to hear it,' Mary said with a rueful grin. 'He really does take a pride in his cooking and loves to hear when people appreciate it.' Mary smiled. 'Oh, did you know that Dr Jardine is here, too?'

For a moment Cenna stared as Mary nodded to a table positioned on a raised dais. Then to her astonishment she

saw Phil sitting at the table. 'Enjoy your meal,' Mary said
as she placed their main courses on the table.

'What's wrong?' Mark asked after she had gone.

'Nothing,' Cenna said, attempting to hide her shock. 'I'm
just surprised to see a colleague of mine, that's all.'

Mark turned around, narrowing his eyes. 'It's your partner, isn't it? Did you know he was eating here tonight?'

Cenna shook her head. 'No, I didn't.'

'He has a very attractive girlfriend,' Mark remarked.
Helen Prior, dressed all in black, looked stunning.

Cenna met Phil's gaze across the room. He seemed to
look at her for a long while and she at him as she gripped
her napkin tightly between her fingers.

'Your partner has good taste,' Mark commented. 'Have
they been going out together long?'

'I've no idea.' Cenna lifted her fork. Her appetite had
vanished. The chicken cooked in a delicious French wine
and herbs was delicious but she barely tasted it. In fact, all
she recalled from the meal was listening to Mark drone on.
But all she could think of was Phil. What was he doing
here? He had said he was going to be busy this evening.
Was Helen his girlfriend as Mark had suggested?

Cenna managed to finish her main course but whilst
Mark went on to devour his *crème brûlée*, she toyed with
hers, her eyes drawn back every so often to the couple
across the room.

'I've enjoyed every mouthful,' Mark said as they ordered
coffee. 'But most of all,' he whispered across the table,
reaching out to grasp her hand, 'I've enjoyed being with
you, Cenna.'

Just then Phil rose from his seat and escorted Helen
across the floor.

'I hope,' Phil said as he arrived at their table, with Helen
at his side, 'your meal was as delicious as ours.'

'It was,' Mark replied.

Helen smiled, then linked her arm through Phil's. Cenna felt a pain inside her that was almost physical. She couldn't believe herself capable of feeling this way and she was aware that the emotion was preventing her from acting normally. Helen made a few passing remarks, but Cenna wasn't listening. Round and round in her mind went the questions, and by the time Phil and Helen said goodbye Cenna was desperate to leave and go home.

When Mark suggested they stop for a drink at the bar afterwards, she refused. She paid for the one meal and hurriedly put on her coat.

'Aren't you going to invite me back for coffee?' Mark asked when they were outside.

'You know that isn't possible,' she told him, and held out her hand. 'Goodbye, Mark.'

'It's him, isn't it?' Mark accused her suddenly. 'I saw it in your eyes when he walked over.'

'Don't be ridiculous, Mark.'

'I'm not. I watched you.'

'Mark, goodnight—'

He pulled her back as she went to walk away. 'You're jealous!' he accused her, his eyes narrowing. 'You're jealous of her.'

Cenna stared at him, humiliated and embarrassed. But she was also very angry. 'Let go of me, Mark.' She pulled away, her heart beating fast as she hurried to her car. Her hands were trembling as she drove away. She could hardly recall driving home, only that she managed to get there eventually.

Once she was in the safety of her kitchen, she sank down on a chair and closed her eyes. What an ugly scene with Mark. Oh, why had she gone this evening? What hurt most was that Mark was right. She had been jealous of Helen. The emotion had overwhelmed her and Mark had guessed.

But it wasn't Mark she spent the next few hours thinking

about. It was Phil. There were no answers to why Phil had chosen to go to the Summerville with Helen other than the obvious one. He'd wanted to be there with her.

As usual, on Monday at lunchtime, the Fisherman's Haunt was busy with local trade. Cenna and Jane took their preferred seat by the window. It was their usual spot, a perfect place to eat a quick lunch.

Jane had married Marcus Granger quietly last year after the discovery of her pregnancy. She now looked blooming in her fifth month. Catching up on their personal news had been almost impossible, Cenna reflected as they ordered sandwiches. Jane's and Marcus's house move from their town centre cottage to a larger house on the outskirts of Nair had left little opportunity for socialising.

'The house needs renovation,' Jane explained as they ate their sandwiches, her blue eyes thoughtful under her silky blonde bob. 'But we'll never get it done before the baby's born.'

'You should try to take things a little easier,' Cenna said in concern.

Jane laughed. 'I'm as strong as a horse.'

'You're also five months pregnant. Why don't you take a little more time off from the surgery?'

Jane pouted. 'I'm only part time now. And, besides, I'll have plenty of time after the baby's born.'

'Don't be so sure.' Cenna's smile was rueful. 'You may have a very active baby.'

'Well, I'll have Ben to help me. He's as excited as we are.'

Cenna knew that Jane was deliriously happy. Meeting Marcus again after many years had rekindled their love and Ben, Marcus's stepson from his first marriage, was a happy, well-adjusted seven-year-old. Cenna adored him. And with his brother or sister due to arrive in May, the family circle would be complete.

Jane sat back on her chair, laying her hand gently on the small bump under her smart grey maternity suit. 'Cenna, sometimes I can't believe we're so lucky.'

'You waited a long time for each other,' Cenna remarked softly. 'You deserve to be happy.'

'And what about you?' Jane asked with a wry smile. 'I saw a rather good-looking young man in Reception with you a little while ago...'

'I expect you mean Mark Paget,' Cenna said crisply. 'We lived in the same town in the north—he looked me up when he brought his mother down to Southampton last Christmas.'

'You dated each other?' Jane asked.

Cenna nodded. 'Yes, but he met someone else. I think I could have coped with that—if he'd told me. But he didn't. I found out through a friend.'

'That must have hurt,' Jane said softly.

'At the time, it did. But I realised when I moved to Nair just how little Mark and I had in common.'

There was a pause before Jane asked slowly, 'I take it that you and Phil haven't spent any time together?'

The answer to that was, of course, no. As she gazed into the enquiring depths of her friend's blue eyes, Cenna recalled she had shared her confused feelings with Jane after the party last year.

'No...we haven't,' Cenna answered with a shrug. 'As a matter of fact, I went with Mark to the Summerville on Saturday evening.'

'The Summerville?' Jane repeated in surprise.

Cenna nodded. 'Mark said he was leaving England and that he would like to part good friends. Foolishly I agreed to meet him, but it was a dreadful mistake. Phil and Helen were eating there and it was all very embarrassing.'

Cenna was surprised when Jane smiled. 'Oh, I think I can explain that. Phil offered Marcus and me the tickets, but I had to refuse at the last moment because of Ben's friend staying over. Helen was there and—well, she said she liked French food...'

'You mean Phil didn't ask her out?'

Jane shook her head. 'No, that wasn't my impression at all.'

'Phil said he was busy on Saturday night,' Cenna murmured, her brow creased. 'And that he was offering the tickets to you.'

'Yes, he did.' Jane shrugged. 'Something must have cropped up to make him change his plans because I'm certain he wouldn't have told you a lie.'

Cenna wondered if it was a demure brunette in a little black number that had caused Phil to think again. 'I don't know,' she sighed in confusion. 'Jane, I don't know what to think any more.'

'Has he talked about Helen—I mean, said anything at all?'

'No. It was Mark who commented they looked the happy couple, and I have to agree—they did.'

'Looks aren't everything,' Jane said reasonably. 'After all, I expect the same might be said of you and Mark.'

'You mean Phil might have thought...' Cenna's voice tailed off. Jane had a point, she supposed, but her reasons for going out with Mark had been genuine. She simply couldn't believe that Phil and Helen had been there for any reason other than to enjoy themselves.

'Why don't you simply ask Phil if he's going out with Helen?' Jane suggested easily.

Cenna couldn't help but smile. Jane made it sound so easy.

'Nothing ventured, nothing gained,' Jane prompted as

the clock over the bar struck two, the signal for their return
to surgery.

Breathing in the fresh salt air cutting across the car park,
Cenna wondered what Phil would say if she asked him if
he was seeing Helen. As she parted from Jane, Cenna realised she didn't want to know. She didn't want to look in
Phil's eyes as he gave her the answer she didn't want
to hear.

CHAPTER THREE

'DID you enjoy yourselves on Saturday evening?' Phil asked as he met Cenna in the corridor of the surgery on Monday afternoon.

It was a pleasant enough enquiry, yet there was an edge to his voice that she didn't recognise. 'Yes,' she answered briefly. 'And you?'

'The food was first class.' He added quickly, 'As you know, I didn't intend to eat out, but—'

'But plans can change at a moment's notice?' she interrupted him.

'Yes, as it happens, they did,' Phil answered in tones that mirrored her own.

Damn it, she thought. This wasn't supposed to happen. She had planned a few flippant remarks—comments on the food at the Summerville and so forth. Now they were closer to arguing than holding a conversation.

They were silent for a long moment, apparently with little to say to each other. Then Phil gave his usual shrug, commenting he had better let her get to surgery. She remarked that she was indeed rather late and moved quickly away. But in her room she sank down on her chair with a dismayed sigh. She was still no closer to knowing whether Phil and Helen were dating.

Why did his offhand attitude hurt so much and why had she retaliated in such a way? If only she hadn't thought of the ridiculous idea of asking Mark to eat with her at the Summerville! What could have possessed her? And yet if she hadn't seen Phil and Helen together, she might very well have made a fool of herself at a later date. This conclusion gave her a small measure of comfort as she sat, trying to assemble her thoughts.

Attempting to return her mind to her patients, she told herself that things might improve between them as the week went on.

But they didn't.

Instead, they got worse.

By Friday, it was panic stations. A flu bug felled many and those who managed to attend surgery were coughing, sneezing and irritable and Cenna had barely spoken more than a few words to Phil all week. The sickness, diarrhoea and temperature, which had first afflicted only a few, progressed steadily; tempers were especially frayed amongst those families involved in the fishing industry. If the men couldn't go out in the boats, the local economy suffered.

'It's another house call,' Annie told Cenna as she was about to leave on Friday evening for her calls. 'Clyde Oakman, the fisherman. He has the bug. And there's Louise Ryman with stomach pain, too. Maybe that's another case of the virus.'

'Perhaps. I did think she might have an anaemia problem, but her blood test results were OK. Put them both down for calls, will you?'

It was half past six before Cenna arrived at the Oakmans' terraced house by the harbour. Della Oakman, Clyde's wife, showed her upstairs to where Clyde lay in bed. A big man with auburn hair and a rugged complexion, he was rarely sick and as she walked in he looked very sorry for himself.

'Can't stay in bed like this—got to open the shop,' he complained as Cenna examined him and confirmed him as yet another victim of flu.

'Well, you won't be able to for a few days,' Cenna answered firmly, suggesting he take paracetamol.

'Paracetamol!' Clyde exclaimed. 'That stuff's not going to do me any good. I need something stronger.'

'It will help to bring down your temperature. Rest and fluids are what you need until the virus has decided it's had enough of you,' Cenna argued lightly, aware that Clyde had recently bought the lease of the seafood shop on the harbour.

'Oh, don't pay any attention to him,' Della told Cenna as they went downstairs. 'He's a terrible patient. Steve, our eldest son, can open the shop. He's out of work at the moment. It will give him something to do.'

'And a damn fine mess he'll make of it,' Clyde shouted from the bedroom. 'Wouldn't know a prawn from an octopus, the big lummock.'

'Clyde thinks he's indispensable,' Della commented as she saw Cenna out. 'Steve won't think much of the idea either, but he'll do it. Clyde's right about one thing—Steve hates fishing and everything to do with the trade. But there you are, needs must, as they say. Ah, here he is now.'

A tall, good-looking young man in a suit strode up the garden path. Like his father, he was well built and auburn-haired.

'Any luck with the job interview?' Della asked.

Her son shrugged. 'I'll have to wait and see. There were other candidates—some of them with more experience than me. Even so, I reckon I could do the job.'

'Steve's a software writer,' Della explained proudly. 'Not that either me or his dad knows what he's talking about sometimes.'

Steve laughed. 'Don't worry, Mum, you don't need to know. How's Dad?'

She grimaced. 'He's confined to bed for a few days,' Della said with a sigh. ''Fraid you'll have to open the shop, Steve.'

'That'll break his heart,' Steve commented wryly.

Della glanced at Cenna. 'He's right. It probably will.'

'What sort of work are you looking for?' Cenna asked interestedly.

'I've a degree in computer science,' Steve told her, 'but unfortunately these days a degree doesn't automatically qualify you for work.'

On her way to visit Louise Ryman, Cenna had a chance to reflect on the plight of the fishing trade in Nair. Only last year Brian Porcher had sold his boats and left the sea. The Porcher family went back generations as fishermen and their exit from the trade had served to highlight the decline in the fishing fleet. Young people often preferred jobs with security and prospects. A few sons followed their fathers to sea, but Nair had seen a shift in attitudes in the past few years.

It was a thought that was still on her mind as she drove through the town centre, past the small guesthouses and hotels preparing for summer visitors. At least Clyde would be able to rely on this source of revenue for his shop.

A few streets on Cenna turned towards Louise Ryman's house, one of a row of Victorian houses in a small cul-de-sac. After several knocks, Louise answered the door and Cenna saw at once that she was ill. 'How long have you been like this?' she asked as Louise sank down on the sofa.

'The pains started in the night. I thought it might be the tummy bug that everyone seems to have. But this morning it's more down here, on my right side.'

Louise lay back on the sofa as Cenna made her examination, groaning as a spasm of pain went through her.

'I feel sick and hot,' Louise said weakly. 'And the pain seems to be getting worse. Is it my appendix, do you think?'

'Perhaps,' Cenna agreed. 'Your pulse and temperature are raised and I'll need to get you into hospital to find out more.'

Louise nodded, tears filling her eyes. 'I...I've missed a period. But I put it down to the tiredness and I'm not all that regular anyway.'

'Are you saying you may be pregnant?'

Louise nodded, her eyes filling with tears.

'I see,' Cenna replied gently. 'Well, all the more reason to investigate further, Louise.' Her fears were growing that Louise had an ectopic pregnancy. 'I'll ring for an ambulance and we'll get you into hospital.'

Cenna finally made the telephone call to Nair Cottage Hospital, only a short distance away. Southampton was too far in this instance—and if the problem was what she suspected, Louise would require swift attention. 'Is there anyone I can contact that you might like to be with you?' she asked when she came back into the room.

'No,' Louise whispered. 'No one, thanks.'

Cenna nodded and whilst she was collecting a few personal items together for Louise to take with her, she was relieved to hear the ambulance siren. As Louise was transported to the ambulance, Cenna wondered what lay behind the unhappy state of affairs. If the father was the man Louise had just parted from then the blow for her must be a double one. And what was even sadder was that there appeared to be no one in whom her young patient could confide.

As Cenna left her room on Wednesday lunchtime, Annie hurried towards her. 'Oh, Dr Lloyd,' she said quickly, 'I wonder if you would like to come to a barbecue. I know it's rather early in the year, but I'm trying to raise some money for Callum's school.'

'If I'm not on call,' Cenna hesitated, 'I'll try to come.'

'Great. We're organising a treasure hunt. The school has offered a prize and we're starting off in their grounds, finally to end up in our garden.' She laughed. 'So, you see, it's all in a good cause.'

Later that day Cenna found herself sharing a pot of coffee in the staffroom with Marcus and Jane when the topic of the barbecue arose again.

'Did Annie mention a barbecue and treasure hunt at Nair Senior?' Marcus asked Cenna as he poured himself a coffee.

'Yes, she did. Are you going?'

He grinned at his wife who was sipping a glass of water. 'Ben is in the primary school still, but it's possible he'll be going on to the seniors, so Jane's going to the barbecue. I've forbidden her to rush around any more than necessary. Ben can haul Darren along with him to the treasure hunt.'

'I wish—' Jane pouted '—you wouldn't fuss. I'm perfectly fit and I'd love to be with Ben on the treas—'

But one look from her husband silenced her and she grimaced at Jane.

'She's doing far too much,' Marcus remarked with a smile that could hardly be called reproving. 'Although she thinks I'm not aware of what goes on behind my back.'

They all laughed at this, but Cenna agreed with Marcus. Jane did take on too much and from what she had said about the house, Cenna knew that Jane's active enthusiasm for its redecoration had known few limits.

'As for me, according to the rota, I'm on call that night.' Marcus sighed. 'So I shall leave you, Cenna, to keep a watchful eye on my wife.'

Cenna gave a rueful smile. 'I'll try my best.' As they laughed again, Cenna glanced at Jane.

'Did you talk to Phil?' Jane asked curiously.

It was a question Cenna had hoped to avoid. 'Well…yes, I did in the end,' she admitted reluctantly.

At this Marcus stood up. 'As much as I'd like to stay and listen to all the news,' he said as he swallowed the last of his coffee, 'I'm collecting Ben from school and I have a call to make beforehand.' He lowered his mug into the sink and quickly washed it, then, turning back, he lifted his case. 'See you later, darling. Bye, Cenna.'

They watched him rush off, then Jane turned slowly and, grinning, raised an eyebrow. 'Well, what did he say?' Jane stared eagerly at her, resting her hand on the bump hidden discreetly under her deep blue dress.

'Nothing much. Just that his plans had changed on Saturday night,' Cenna attempted to explain.

'So you don't know if he is going out with Helen?'

'No.'

Jane sighed. 'Well, just another of life's little mysteries, I suppose.' She shrugged, her brow set in a puzzled frown. 'Perhaps they were discussing work.'

'Work of an intimate nature,' Cenna responded dryly.

'Well, as I said, no doubt you and Mark looked like a couple.'

Cenna raised her eyes. 'Heavens, I hope not.'

It was then that Phil himself entered and Jane glanced at Cenna. 'Well, sitting here all day isn't going to help reduce my list,' she said quickly, rising slowly to her feet. 'Phil, there's a coffee still hot in the percolator. And you might find a few digestives in the cupboard.'

'Oh…thanks, Jane.' Phil smiled and walked over to pour himself a coffee.

'See you both later.' Jane glanced quickly at Cenna who realised that her friend was making a discreet exit.

The atmosphere was tense as Jane glanced at Phil's broad-shouldered back. She was surprised when he turned and said suddenly, 'Did I interrupt something, by any chance?'

'No—why would you think that?'

He sat beside her on the chair Jane had vacated and slowly lowered his mug to the table. 'It's just that we haven't really spoken of late. I've had the feeling you've been avoiding me.'

She met his gaze and, knowing that what he said was true, looked quickly away.

'Is it because of Mark?' he persisted, frowning at her.

She looked sharply up. 'Mark? What do you mean?'

He shrugged. 'I don't know. But it's since Saturday that you've seemed rather distant.'

'I was thinking the same myself,' Cenna replied, 'of you.'

'Oh,' he murmured, and crooked an eyebrow. 'Two minds with but a single thought, it appears.'

'I have to admit,' she added hurriedly, 'that I was surprised to see you at the Summerville. When I first spoke to you about the invitations, you said you would be too busy to go.'

'Yes, that's true,' he agreed. 'I'd made plans to drive to Oxfordshire to visit Maggie's parents. But the trip was called off at the last moment and then—'

'Helen stepped in,' Cenna heard herself saying.

He frowned at her. 'Yes, that's right.' He ran a strong brown finger around the rim of his mug. 'I must admit I was very surprised to see you and Mark there. You looked very…intense.'

'Intense?' Cenna stared at him. 'What do you mean?'

He arched an eyebrow. 'He obviously still has feelings for you,' Phil said, and she stared at him.

'No, not at all.'

'Then I'm surprised.'

'I saw Mark at Christmas,' she found herself explaining, 'when he brought his mother to visit a relative in Southampton. Mrs Paget was a great friend of my mother's. But since then, well…I wish I had never agreed to the meeting. Mark got the wrong impression—'

'And he reappeared at the surgery?' he suggested for her.

Cenna nodded. 'Saturday's meal was a kind of goodbye. Mark is moving to America.'

After a long pause, a soft smile touched his lips. 'Well, we seem to have got all that sorted out,' he sighed. 'Surprising how two little tickets can make life very confusing…'

She smiled and the tension was broken as John Hill, the newest doctor to the group, came in. He gave them a beaming smile, rubbing his hands together. 'Hi, everyone. Any coffee left?'

'Plenty, help yourself,' Phil said, glancing at Cenna.

After a brief chat with John, she left them to finish their coffee and five minutes later was back in her room. Going to the window, she stared thoughtfully over the car park. Did she believe Phil when he said he had been going to Oxford and his plans were cancelled at the last minute? Whether she did or not, it was a question that preoccupied her for the rest of the day.

The following week Homer Pomeroy rang Reception to explain he was unable to keep his afternoon appointment.

'He sounded very odd,' Annie said as she put the phone down and turned to Cenna who had just entered the office. 'When I asked him if he would like a visit from the doctor, he mumbled something—I couldn't tell what—then the line went dead.'

'I think I had better call,' Cenna agreed as she glanced at her watch. 'He was due to come in for a BP check today—I had asked him to come in specifically. I've a blood report that I'd like to discuss with him. Would you sort it out for me, Annie, please?'

On her drive out to Homer's, Cenna wondered why his fiancée had been unable to drive him into surgery. As she rang the doorbell there was no sign of either Homer or his fiancée, but the imposing door of the country house was opened by a small woman dressed in an overall.

'I'm Dr Lloyd,' Cenna introduced herself. 'Is Mr Pomeroy in?'

'Thank goodness you've come,' the woman said, stepping back to allow Cenna in. 'I'm Mrs Vine, his housekeeper. I arrived this morning and found him still in bed. I took him some breakfast, but he said he wasn't feeling very well.' Mrs Vine beckoned as she ascended the staircase. 'I can't get him to answer me now. And I heard a bump in there a few minutes ago. He can't go on like this, you know. One day he'll have a real accident.'

As Cenna followed up the elegant staircase she listened to Mrs Vine explain that her employer had recently quarrelled with his fiancée and was suffering the after-effects of a drinking spree.

'Why don't you try?' Mrs Vine gestured along a thickly carpeted hall. 'Third door on the right.'

Cenna went along and tapped on the door but received no reply. However, when she called her name there was movement from inside and the door finally opened. The room was dark, but it was clear that Homer, dressed in his pyjamas, was having difficulty in standing.

'It's my arthritis,' he complained bitterly. 'Damn useless leg.'

'Hold onto me,' Cenna said as the housekeeper drew the curtains and light flooded the room.

'I'll help you get him comfy,' Mrs Vine offered, and between them they managed to support Homer's considerable weight to the bed.

'Good riddance to bad rubbish,' Mrs Vine remarked loudly as Cenna opened her case. 'She just twists him round her little finger—'

'I wonder if you could ring the surgery for me, Mrs Vine?' Cenna interrupted as she took out her stethoscope and sphygmomanometer. 'Let them know I shall probably be a little late for afternoon surgery.' She gave the number to Mrs Vine who reluctantly left the room.

'Edith's a treasure,' Homer muttered as Cenna began to make her examination, 'but a little strait-laced. In fact, she—'

'Your housekeeper thought she heard a bump,' Cenna interrupted tactfully. 'Did you fall?'

'No, I did not.'

'But you're very unsteady on your legs.'

'Nothing to speak of really—'

'Mr Pomeroy, as you won't come to see me I came to talk to you.'

Homer managed a grin. 'If Mohammed won't come to the mountain, eh?'

'Something like that.' Cenna nodded as she concluded her examination. After she was finished, she sat down on a chair next to the bed.

'I know what you're going to say,' Homer said at once. 'You're going to tear me off a strip.'

'I don't think it would help if I did.' Cenna raised an eyebrow. 'I think you know that if you carry on like this, there can only be one outcome.'

There was silence and Homer sank back on his pillows, closing his eyes. 'The report shows that the level of uric acid in your blood is very high. If you don't begin to take your condition seriously, your blood pressure will continue to rise. This will result in many problems, not the least of which is kidney disease.'

'So what have I got to do?' Homer sighed.

'Take your medication regularly, avoid all foods high in purine. But, most of all, avoid or at least limit your consumption of alcohol.'

The reaction was as she'd expected, a disgruntled moan from her patient, but at least he didn't flatly refuse to cooperate. Just then there was a knock on the door and Mrs Vine called from outside, 'Another visitor.'

'Place is like Piccadilly Circus,' complained Homer as Cenna rose went to the door and opened it. To her surprise, as Mrs Vine left, a familiar tall, dark-haired figure was walking towards her.

'Cenna? Is everything all right?' Phil asked anxiously.

She nodded in surprise as she stepped out into the corridor. 'Yes, but what are you doing here?

'I was in the office when your message came in.' He lowered his voice, peering over her shoulder. 'Mrs Vine told Annie there was trouble and alcohol was involved. I thought I had better check the situation out.' Suddenly he looked embarrassed. 'Her message was quite graphic. Naturally, I was…er…rather anxious.'

'Oh.' Cenna sighed. 'I'm sorry—I should have phoned the surgery myself. Mrs Vine has a rather colourful turn of phrase.'

'Who is it?' came a shout from the bedroom.

Cenna raised her eyebrows. 'It's Dr Jardine.'

'Well, don't stand out there—come in,' Homer called.

Allowing herself a grin, Cenna motioned Phil to enter.

Homer embarked on a series of complaints about his poor health, which he still refused to accept as the result of heavy drinking. Phil listened patiently for a moment or two, then asked if Homer was aware of the concern he had caused everyone, not the least his housekeeper and GP.

This appeared to have some effect as Homer looked duly admonished. But by the time they left, Cenna was still unconvinced of her patient's change of heart and she remarked on this to Phil.

'I think today's events are a result of the article in the *Evening Echo* last night,' Phil replied. 'Did you read it?'

Cenna stopped at her car and frowned. 'No.'

'Apparently Homer and his fiancée had a fight at The

Spyglass. Things turned a bit nasty apparently. A younger man was involved and Homer took a swipe at him. There was talk of an assault charge being made.'

'Oh, that's sad.' Cenna glanced back at the elegant house and well-kept gardens. 'He must think a great deal of her.'

'You mean his young fiancée?' Phil said ruefully as he looked back, too.

'Mrs Vine said she meant the world to him.'

There was a pause as Phil's face suddenly darkened. 'In my opinion it's better this happened now rather than later.'

Cenna frowned. 'You mean you don't think they're suited?'

'Do you?'

'Well...I'm not sure... There's an age gap, I'll agree, but many marriages are successful despite the difference in ages.'

He looked at her for a long time, then shook his head slowly. 'Oh, don't listen to me,' he said, heaving a sigh. 'I'm certain I'm the last person to comment on romance.' He glanced down at her and softly touched her arm. 'You're OK, I take it?'

She nodded. 'Yes, fine. And...thanks, Phil. I appreciate you driving out here on my behalf.'

'I was concerned for a very valued member of staff,' he told her as their eyes met.

A few seconds later they parted, and as she watched his car disappeared from view. Is that how he thought of her—'a very valued member of staff'? She should be flattered, but instead a familiar ache of dismay engulfed her.

CHAPTER FOUR

IT WAS quite a few weeks later when Cenna received notification from Nair Cottage Hospital that Louise Ryman had suffered an ectopic pregnancy. On Saturday morning, after her emergency surgery, she called at Louise's house.

When she arrived there, the curtains were still drawn. However, her knock brought Louise to the glass-fronted Victorian door and, though fully dressed, she looked very pale.

'Hello, Louise.' Cenna glanced into the gloomy hall. 'How are you?'

After a moment or two Louise stepped back and gestured her to enter. 'I'm OK, I suppose.'

The place was cold and smelt rather musty as they walked into the front room. Louise drew the curtains, revealing the sight of two pillows and a duvet on one of the chairs.

'Sorry, I've been sleeping downstairs and it's a bit of a mess,' Louise apologised, removing them in order that Cenna could sit down. 'I haven't felt much like housework even though I haven't been back to school. I just haven't got the energy.'

'It will take a while to get back on your feet,' Cenna said quietly as Louise sank down onto the sofa.

Louise looked at Cenna. 'The surgeon had to remove one of my Fallopian tubes,' she murmured. 'He couldn't repair it properly.'

Cenna nodded. 'Yes, but it will still be possible for you to have a normal pregnancy.'

'That seems hardly likely now,' Louise answered tightly.

'Martin has left me and gone back to his wife. So becoming pregnant again is out of the question.'

'For now, yes,' Cenna agreed, 'but you're still young, Louise. You'll meet someone else in due course.'

Louise fumbled for a tissue and blew her nose. 'You don't understand. I was in love with Martin. He said his marriage was over and I thought he loved me, too. I can't help thinking if I'd had the baby, he would have come back to me.' Louise held her head in her hands. 'I feel so depressed.'

'I could give you something to help...' Cenna hesitated '...but it would be better if you had someone to talk to—perhaps a girlfriend who understands the situation.'

Louise shrugged. 'You don't keep many friends in a job like mine when you're having an affair. But I do have a friend from college—I could ask her to spend a few days with me.'

'Why don't you do that?' Cenna encouraged. 'Then come and see me next week and we'll talk again.' Cenna completed the sickness certificate and handed it to Louise.

'Thanks. I'll ring Sally tonight.'

Cenna was still thinking of Louise as she arrived home and walked into her bright, modern house. Louise would find her own way as she recovered both emotionally and physically from her affair with the married man. But Cenna suspected that it wasn't going to be easy for Louise. Cutting herself off socially wouldn't aid the healing process.

Her thoughts were interrupted by the phone ringing in the kitchen. She hurried to answer it. 'You haven't forgotten the barbecue tonight, have you, Dr Lloyd?' Annie asked worriedly. 'Lots of people seem to have gone away for Easter. I'm desperate we won't get enough numbers.'

'Yes, I'm still coming.' Cenna hid her sigh. She could think of better things to do after the week she'd had—like a long, luxurious bath and curling up on the sofa with a book. 'What time, Annie?'

'The treasure hunt is at six, starting off at the school. And the barbecue at eight, here at my house.'

'OK. I'll probably make the barbecue.'

'Brilliant. See you then. Oh, and dress up warmly—and throw on some insect repellent. They're out in their hordes.'

Cenna put down the phone and mentally rummaged through her wardrobe. Now she had to think of something to wear, discover where she had hidden the mosquito repellent and unearth a bottle of wine from the fridge.

Cenna opted for jeans and a warm sweater since the nights were still cool. She wanted an excuse to break in the new jeans and the luxurious deep green cable-stitch sweater with its thick rollneck, which would keep out any night-time chill. She pinned her dark hair up into a fashionable clip and decided on trainers as opposed to sandals—just in case there were games for the kids that the grown-ups might be hauled into.

With a last glance in the mirror, she recalled she had a bottle of red wine in the rack and stowed it in the car along with a bumper packet of crisps.

Annie and Mike Sharpe's house was large and rambling and Callum and Michael, their two boys of thirteen and ten, were in the front garden directing visitors as Cenna drove up. The house was floodlit with outside lamps and fairy lights, giving the evening more of a Christmassy feel than late spring.

Cenna had visited once or twice before but only briefly, and as she parked her car on the opposite side of the wide road, she saw Marcus, Jane and Ben arrive in their car. Soon they were all laughing and talking as they met up on the front lawn. Ben had come second in the treasure hunt with his friend Darren and was immediately whisked off by Michael Sharpe. Marcus was on call and didn't stay, but Jane and Cenna walked slowly into the rear garden together.

The music from the stereo was playing across the lawn and groups of people scattered around the big garden were already eating sausages and kebabs.

'Great to see you,' Annie called as Jane and Cenna approached the stone-built barbecue where Mike Sharpe, dressed in a striped apron, was chef for the evening. 'Congratulations to Ben and Darren,' Mike shouted as Cenna handed over the wine and crisps. 'Come and fill your plates before the crowds get here.'

Jane did so, at the same time talking to John Hill and his wife and several girls from Reception.

'Everyone's here—almost,' Annie was saying, batting away the mosquitoes. 'Do you know if Dr Jardine's coming? Or is he doing something else?'

Cenna shook her head. She had wondered the same herself but hadn't had the time—or the nerve—to ask Phil. She avoided Annie's frown of curiosity as she harpooned the sausages Mike had tipped on to her plate. Phil hadn't mentioned the barbecue and it was with a sense of disappointment that she assumed he was probably avoiding it.

Leaving the barbecue and finding a space for herself and Jane at a table, she glanced at a white-faced Jane. 'Hey, what's up? You look shattered.'

'It's been a frantic day with the boys and last-minute shopping,' Jane said in a shaky voice. 'And unfortunately Marcus has been on call so—' Jane stopped and grasped her bump. 'Oh, no… I can't believe it.'

'What's the matter—is it the baby?'

Jane closed her eyes and took a breath. 'I think I'm starting contractions. I had a mild one as I was standing by the barbecue.'

'How far on are you?'

Jane swallowed. 'Not quite eight months.'

'Let me ring Marcus,' Cenna said at once, standing up.

'No…not until I'm sure.' She held her head in her hands.

Cenna was worried as she sat down again. 'Jane, if you're having contractions and the baby is early…'

'I know, I know.' Jane looked white. As doctors, they both knew something was wrong and even if the pains weren't contractions, Jane still needed to be examined. Cenna didn't want to alarm her friend, neither did she wish to delay—and she wasn't certain if Jane was telling her the truth about the number of contractions she'd had.

Jane shivered, even though she was dressed warmly in coat and trousers.

'Look, I'm going to ring Marcus—'

'No!' Jane grasped her wrist. 'Please, wait, Cenna. I don't want to alarm Marcus, or Ben—if it's not the real thing.'

Jane was about to protest when a tall figure balancing a plate of kebabs pushed his way through the crowd. Dressed in jeans and a dark sweater, Phil grinned as he approached. 'Hi, there.' He smiled as he pulled out a chair and sat down, placing his plate on the table. 'Mind if I join—?' He stopped in mid-sentence as he glanced at their faces. 'What's wrong?' His frown deepened as he stared at them.

Quite suddenly Jane gave a small groan and, leaning forward, Cenna saw pain written in her eyes.

'Is it the baby?' Phil's voice was calm, but Cenna nodded and he stood up, going quickly around to Jane. 'Do you think you can make the house?'

After a moment, Jane nodded. Phil took one arm and helped her to stand and Cenna took the other arm. Fortunately they were close to the French doors of the house and few noticed Jane's distress as they helped her inside. However, when they entered the large room, Ben was playing on the computer with Michael.

'What's the matter?' Ben asked, looking anxious.

'I'm going to have a rest for a few moments,' Jane told him as he came to stand beside her.

'Can I come with you?' Ben stared at his stepmother in alarm.

'Mum is going to lie down,' Cenna said gently, understanding the look of entreaty that Jane had given her. 'Perhaps we could make her a cup of tea?'

This suggestion seemed to reassure Ben who followed Cenna to the kitchen, whilst Phil helped Jane from the room.

A few minutes later, Cenna was still trying to keep Ben occupied in the kitchen when Phil appeared. Attempting not to alarm the child, he indicated to Cenna that he was about to use the cellphone lying on the worktop.

'She's in labour,' he told her quietly out of ear shot of Ben. 'And there's no time to lose.'

Later that evening, Phil tiredly lifted the large tabby cat from his lap and lowered him gently to the floor.

'Can Donovan sleep on my bed tonight?' Ben asked as, freshly washed and scrubbed, he stood in his pyjamas in the large, warm drawing room of Jane's and Marcus's home.

Phil nodded, drawing the boy down onto the sofa. 'I'm sure he can. How was the bath?'

'OK. Do you have to go out to see any patients?'

'No,' Phil said gently. 'Neither of us do.'

'When will Mummy be home?'

'As soon as she's feeling better.'

'Will she bring the baby with her?'

There was a moment's pause before Phil managed to change the subject and Cenna, listening to the conversation as she walked through from the hall, smiled at them both. The sight of Phil sprawled on the large, chintzy sofa, his arm around the boy's shoulders, comforted her and she knew that he was making every effort to sound normal for Ben's sake. But she could see the strain in his eyes and feared that it would be a long night ahead.

She sat beside them, her hand going down to stroke the purring cat trailing its supple body around her ankles. 'So…where does Donovan usually sleep?' she asked in an attempt to distract Ben's thoughts.

'In the kitchen, but sometimes, if it's really cold, Mum lets him sleep on the end of my bed.'

Cenna met Phil's weary but amused gaze. 'I'm sure he'd enjoy a treat. I know where I'd rather sleep if I had the choice.'

'Are you both going to sleep here tonight?'

Phil glanced at Cenna. 'Well, that depends.'

'On if my dad comes home from the hospital?'

Phil nodded.

'What if he doesn't?'

'Cenna is going to stay—'

'But we've got loads of bedrooms.'

Cenna didn't know what to say. Everything had happened so quickly at the barbecue. Her priority had been Ben, making certain he'd stayed with her and that she'd answered his questions as best she could, whilst Phil had attended to Jane. Hurriedly they'd assured Jane as she'd gone into the ambulance that they would take care of Ben. When Marcus had arrived, just before the ambulance had driven off, there had only been time for Marcus to give them the keys of the house.

'Would you feel better if both of us were here?' she asked Ben.

Without hesitation he nodded and Phil ruffled the damp, dark mop of hair.

'OK.' Phil grinned. 'You'd better show me around, just so I don't walk into any cupboards in the night.'

Ben jumped off his lap. 'Can we watch television for a bit?'

Phil chuckled. 'Not at midnight we can't.'

Ben yawned. 'I haven't got school tomorrow. It's Sunday.'

'Whoopee,' said Phil with a grin at Cenna. 'Just as long as you aren't up at the crack of dawn.'

'I'm usually awake by seven o'clock,' Ben said, gripping the big hand that curled around his. 'Or sometimes six.'

'Heck,' groaned Phil. 'On *Sunday*?'

Ben burst out laughing. 'Only joking.'

'Don't I get a hug?' Cenna called, and was rewarded by a bear hug before Ben ran back to join Phil and ascend the stairs.

'I'll be up to say goodnight in a little while,' Cenna called after them.

In the silence of the room, Cenna sat back on the sofa and let out a long sigh. Somehow they had managed to keep positive. Jane had been distraught over Ben. They had promised her they would do all they could to reassure him. This included Cenna staying the night at the Grangers' house. Now all they could do was wait and hope. Marcus would ring, but when they had no idea. And what was worse, they both knew the potential of Jane's condition.

A little while later, she heard Phil coming down the stairs. He walked into the drawing room, his long legs encased in jeans, his tall, supple body moving slowly across the floor to collapse beside her on the sofa. They had both removed their heavy sweaters and wore shirts, the blazing natural gas fire sending out waves of warmth across the room.

'How was he?' she asked, suddenly aware of his presence beside her. Despite her tiredness, a shiver went through her as his arm brushed hers.

'Pretty good on the whole.' Phil thrust a hand through

his dark hair, his broad shoulders rising under the blue cotton shirt, and again she keenly felt his presence. 'I've been given my quarters, the bedroom opposite. You're in the one next door, apparently.'

She grinned. 'I'll make up the beds later. Coffee?'

'No. No…just sit down for a while. You've been on the go all night.'

'I'm out of practice,' she admitted. 'He was quite specific about not being ogled in the bath.'

'A young man's modesty starts early these days.' Then his smile faded as he looked at her. 'He's concerned about Jane. Worried sick, in fact.'

'I know.'

'Marcus said he thinks it's because his natural mother died when he was too young to remember her—and now he's worried about Jane going away, too.' He crooked an eyebrow. 'Let's just hope—'

'That everything's all right.'

They were silent then, deep in their own thoughts. Cenna felt that shiver inside again as she realised that although she had known Phil for nearly four years she had never really been entirely alone with him outside work. Last year, at the party at her house, had been the first time. She remembered it so clearly. And again her skin trembled at the thought.

'This house is huge, isn't it?' she said, knowing she was babbling. 'A perfect house for a family to grow up in. The kind you read about in magazines. When they've redecorated it will be—' She stopped suddenly, the thought of sleeping in the same house as Phil making the back of her neck prickle ridiculously. Then with a jolt of self-conscious guilt she looked into Phil's amused brown eyes. 'You're laughing at me!'

'No. Not at you.'

'Why, then?'

'Just that you're a natural with kids, did you know that?'

She gazed at him in surprise. 'Am I?'

'Ben worships the ground you walk on. If anyone could comfort him, it's you.'

She laughed in the fire glow, her amber eyes soft and glistening. 'We bonded early, when Marcus and Ben first came to Nair. I've looked after him enough times for him to know I'm not going to leave him.'

'And that's what he's worried about,' Phil said as he relaxed back into the cushions of the sofa, his long legs sprawled out in front of him. 'Though as Marcus said—not that he outwardly shows his concern. But the memory of his mother's illness must still be in that tiny mind somewhere and, of course, he associates anything like tonight with something threatening.'

Cenna nodded. 'He had a short bout of asthma before his bath. The puffer arrested it, thank goodness. When I asked him when he last had an attack, he said he couldn't remember.'

'Marcus mentioned that at the hospital. Apparently for the last six months, Ben hasn't needed the Ventolin. I think after Jane comes home with the baby, things will settle down again.'

'Tell me what happened at the hospital,' Cenna asked as she pushed her dark hair back from her face and curled her long legs under her on the chair. She asked the question that had been on her mind all evening. She was aware that a high percentage of cases of premature labour were caused through high blood pressure and an accumulation of fluid in tissues that sometimes developed in the second half of pregnancy.

'My feeling is that it was her blood pressure,' Phil said darkly. 'By the time we got to the hospital she was feeling pretty sick and had some visual disturbance.'

'Did you speak to the obstetrician?'

He nodded. 'I think probably he'll decide on a Caesar.'

They were silent for a moment, well aware of the complications of Jane's condition and just how much this baby was long awaited. A baby that should have been born a decade ago if Jane and Marcus had been able to marry when they had intended. But fate had caused them to give up their happiness for a mutual friend who'd been dying of leukaemia. Marcus had married her and had looked after her throughout her illness, giving Ben the security of a future. It had been seven years before he'd met Jane again and Cenna had been there to witness the renewal of their love.

'And the baby?'

'Chances are good.' Phil nodded. 'We'll just have to wait and see.'

'Marcus will ring us?'

'He'll ring.' He frowned at her. 'Are you OK? *Really* OK?'

Cenna nodded, folding her arms around herself. Even though it was warm she felt cold inside.

'Here…come closer.' He slid an arm around her and drew her back. She leaned against him, feeling suddenly drained, unable to fight the tiredness. She knew it was shock and the inability to help more.

As she closed her eyes she knew Phil wanted to comfort her. She also knew that he was concerned for her. Any action he made was made for her benefit, her ease and peace of mind. It was because of this she relaxed into his arms, her head fitting neatly into the slope of his broad shoulder and the taut, supportive muscle of his arm.

He smelt of the night, the hospital, the barbecue and a certain something else that drifted into her nostrils and made her stomach lurch. She quietened the emotion, unwilling to allow it to develop, clenching her hands as his fingers slid up and down her arm in a gentle fashion, as though he were comforting a child.

'She will be all right, you know,' he breathed above her. His voice rumbled in his chest under the soft blue cotton of his shirt. His warmth reached her and she closed her eyes as she lay against him.

'They deserve this baby, Phil…it's so important to them.'

'And they'll have it…' But his voice faltered and she knew he was thinking the same, his mind revolving on the facts and the certain knowledge that when the baby was born the possible complications of prematurity were legion. For once she wished she didn't know so much and he read her thoughts as he whispered, 'It might be tough for a little while but, God willing, Jane and the baby will come through all this.'

She realised their thoughts were ranging wildly from one possibility to another, but that always it came back to the bare facts. Of the babies born at twenty-eight weeks, eighty per cent survived with specialist care. And Jane was almost eight months. And most premature babies caught up with full-term babies before the end of the first year.

'She looked so…vulnerable,' Cenna whispered almost to herself as she thought of Jane lying on the stretcher and her brave smile when Marcus had arrived. 'And she insisted on keeping on at work. I don't think she was telling us the truth. You know, I had my suspicions—'

'She *is* a doctor,' Phil reminded her gently.

'And we're often the worst as patients,' she murmured.

He squeezed her arm gently. 'Talking of doctors, don't you think it's time you got some rest, too, Dr Lloyd?'

She began to ease herself up, but his arm came around her and she felt herself tremble. Then something happened so quickly she could never recall afterwards just what. Something, as she turned to smile at him, which made her check herself and stiffen against him, before lifting her eyes.

It was a moment that she would always remember, like a bolt of lightning welding them together as a heat and energy turned her to fire as she gazed into the dark brown eyes that were filled with the same mix of chemistry and need.

The next second splintered, crashing into her ears, so startling she thought it was real. And then she was in his arms, her hands linking around his neck as his lips descended on hers, shockingly, powerfully, with a need that matched the crazy pounding of her heart.

It was no gentle embrace, no kiss of comfort or controlled measure, but an urgent, passionate, breathless kiss that left her gasping, her breath trapped in her throat as she responded, her body leaning into his, burning up in his embrace.

How long it went on she didn't know. It was a kiss that seemed to have been waiting on her lips for an eternity, a sleeping kiss that ignited the patient desire inside her into a fiery furnace. The desire that she had always sought to control and had established, so often, as one-sided on her part. A need that had embarrassed her, deceived her, eluded her. A desire that she had felt guilty about, with Maggie never far from her mind and, she had suspected, never far from his.

When at last Phil prised her away, his cheeks were flushed, his dark eyes filled with another emotion. She was trembling, her body shuddering, and he sat back on the sofa against the cushions.

'Cenna…' His voice was rough and husky, trying to get a grip. 'I…don't know if I should apologise or…' He lowered his head, though his hands still trapped her. Then he looked slowly up and she knew what he had been going to say. She willed him to say it, but he didn't.

Instead he released her, his shoulders hunched under his shirt.

'Phil, I don't want you to apologise.' Her answer surprised her. From somewhere deep down she found the strength to tell him the truth. 'I wanted you to kiss me.'

He looked round slowly, his brown eyes like lasers boring into hers. In their depths she saw his need. As strong as her own. And something inside her snapped with relief.

He shrugged. 'I—I can't say that I tried very hard not to kiss you. But at a time like this—'

'At a time like this, it's very comforting.'

He gave her a lopsided grin. 'I didn't kiss you to comfort you.'

'I know.'

He took her hand, curling it into his large palms, entwining his fingers with hers. They looked at one another for a long while, then he drew her hand up against his cheek, rough with stubble. 'I don't feel as though I should be doing this right now.'

'We aren't doing anything,' she replied, trying to ignore the feeling that she was.

He grinned. 'No, we're not. I think you should go and check Ben. And when you come down, we'll talk.'

He stood, drawing her to her feet. Leaning forward, he brushed her lips lightly with his.

CHAPTER FIVE

WHEN Cenna came downstairs again, Phil was speaking on the phone. She could hear his lowered tones and as she entered the drawing room his broad back was to her. She could see by the tension in his shoulders that it was news from the hospital.

She waited until Marcus spoke, a low grunt that ended with a few words she couldn't make out, then he seemed to sense her presence behind him.

He turned slowly, saying goodbye at the same time. When he had lowered the phone, he looked at her. His face was drawn into gaunt lines. 'Is he asleep?' he asked, and she nodded.

'Fast asleep.'

'Good. Come and sit down.'

She closed the door softly, leaving it open an inch. Then she moved across the room and towards the sofa. He was already there and sank down into the cushions, pushing a hand through his dark hair. The firelight reflected on his blue shirt and the shadow across his jaw made her realise how late it must be.

She sat beside him, close enough to feel his warmth. 'That was Marcus?'

He nodded and, raising a hand to push back a lock of dark hair from her eyes, said gruffly, 'Jane's still in Theatre. There were…some complications.'

Jane looked away. 'Oh, God, poor Marcus.'

'He'll let us know as soon as there's news.'

'Did you tell him we'll stay with Ben?' It was all she could think of to ask.

Phil nodded. 'And he's asked me to sort out the weekend duty. John is doing tonight, but maybe I'll fill in tomorrow. I'll ring him in the morning when I know…' He stopped, looking haggard, then went on, 'When we know more.'

There seemed nothing to say after that and Cenna felt thankful for the hand that gripped her arm, squeezing it gently. Then his hand tipped her chin and he forced her to look at him. In his eyes she glimpsed the tiredness and worry, and the lines of strain around his mouth weren't entirely hidden by a forced smile. Gone was the raging desire that had filled the depths of his brown eyes a while ago. She, too, felt nothing but a numbness now, a shock that clamped her body like a vice.

'Hey, come on, she'll be OK,' he said with more conviction that she felt.

'I hope so, Phil.'

'You're tired. Why don't you go up? I'll sit here for a while and listen for the phone.'

'I don't think I could sleep.' A bone-weary tiredness was filling her, but she knew that if she closed her eyes she would have to force them to stay shut. And in the darkness it would be worse, thoughts milling in her mind that she'd have no control over.

'Then crash here…on the sofa,' he said quietly.

She was grateful for his understanding and leaned on the strong arm that went around her and drew her close. She lay there against him, her mind unwilling to settle.

As his breathing evened out beneath her cheek, so hers did, too. The house was quiet with only the soft hiss of the fire and the occasional creak to disturb the peace. She felt her lids drooping, the motion of his breathing lulling her into a fitful, dream-filled sleep.

It was five to six when something disturbed Cenna. She opened her eyes to the light peeping in through the curtains and the smell of coffee brewing somewhere in the house. A heavy tartan blanket was draped over her legs, her bare toes peeping out from the end of it.

She listened for a while and remembered where she was. She heard the noises coming from the kitchen and recognised the sound of Phil's voice and a lighter one drifting through the hall.

Then a large tabby cat leapt up on her legs and purred noisily into the cushions of the sofa. As he made himself comfortable, purring loudly, she eased herself up into a sitting position.

'Hi, cat,' she muttered groggily, and stretched out to stroke him. Lowering her bare feet to the ground, she yawned, stretched, then recalled everything that had happened. Panic filled her and she jumped up, almost crashing into a small figure in pyjamas.

'Oh, Ben!' She grabbed the mug of tea that she had almost knocked out of his hand. 'Sorry, I nearly sent you flying there!'

The grin was instant and the untroubled dark brown eyes gave her some measure of relief. Common sense told her if something had happened she wouldn't have been allowed to sleep like she had...and Ben wouldn't be here, handing her a mug of tea.

'Morning,' Phil called as he entered the room, clean-shaven and fully dressed.

'You should have woken me,' she burst out, feeling a wreck, her hair a mess and her eyes still filled with sleep.

'No reason to. Well, at least, none that couldn't wait.' He gave her one long glance as he drew the heavy curtains.

Then she was aware of Ben staring at her, bursting to speak.

'What is it?' she asked, suddenly fully awake.

Both of them had grins. Phil's was brave and stage-managed, she suspected, but Ben's was utterly genuine.

'I've got a baby sister,' he said unable to contain himself any longer.

'Oh, Ben—that's wonderful!' Cenna lowered the mug to the coffee-table and pulled him against her. Over his small shoulder she glanced up at Phil and he nodded, but the smile he gave her didn't reach his eyes.

'She's really small yet, so she can't come home,' Ben elaborated, pushing himself away. 'She's got to be…what did you say, Uncle Phil? More than two kilograms…so she can eat properly.'

'That's it,' Phil agreed somewhat over-brightly. 'Two point two five or thereabouts.'

'We haven't got a name for her yet,' Ben added enthusiastically, wrestling with the elastic in his pyjamas. 'But I'm going to think of some to tell Mummy.'

'Good idea,' said Phil, glancing again at Cenna.

'Donovan slept on my bed all night,' Ben informed her, lifting the cat into his arms. 'But now he has to go out in the garden.'

Cenna smiled, eager to know about Jane and the baby yet sensing that Phil didn't want to tell her in front of Ben. 'And I think I'd better shower,' she said quickly, standing up.

'Be our guest.' Phil nodded to the staircase. 'There's towels, toothpaste and a toothbrush in the bathroom.'

'Mummy always keeps new brushes for emergencies,' Ben clarified. 'But the baby won't need one, 'cos she hasn't got any teeth.'

'Slip on some clothes when you've put Donovan outside,' Phil said gently, ushering the boy to the door.

'Can I phone Mummy at the hospital?'

'Yes, just as soon as your dad says.' Phil grinned. 'Now, off you go.'

When Ben had gone, Phil glanced quickly after him then

closed the door. 'Marcus rang at five,' he told her in a low voice. 'There was no point in waking you.'

'And…?'

'They've incubated the baby…she had breathing difficulties. They're also concerned about jaundice.'

'They're feeding her intravenously?'

Phil nodded slowly. 'She'll be OK.'

'And Jane?'

He paused, his jaw tightening. 'They did a Caesar but she's had a rough time—complications caused by high blood pressure. I told Marcus he was to stay at the hospital as long as he's needed.'

She opened her mouth to ask more then knew there was nothing sensible she could say. There was no point in asking questions. Not yet. They just had to pray that Jane and the baby would recover.

Phil bent and pushed the hot mug of tea into her hands. She knew she looked dreadful, her hair all over the place, her body stiff and aching from a restless night's sleep on the sofa. 'Drink this,' he told her firmly, 'then have that shower. You'll feel better afterwards. Then we'll eat, fortify ourselves for the day ahead.'

She looked up at him, squirming at the mention of food. 'I don't feel I can face breakfast just yet.'

He grinned and wagged a finger. 'Never quarrel with the chef.' Then, with a brief touch of his hand on her hair, he was gone.

Cenna knew that something had changed inside her. She was fighting it, resisting the feelings that were growing stronger. She didn't want to think about what was happening to her, yet she must. She had to look deeper inside herself as her feelings for Phil grew. And what she found there disturbed her. The emotions that caused her most pain were those connected to Helen Prior. It was no use attempting to deny it. Jealousy was a terrible thing and festered if hidden away. Phil hadn't spoken of Helen, yet was she in his thoughts? She so looked like Maggie. And it was this resemblance, Cenna realised, that underpinned all her fears.

With two doctors short, the three of them—she, Phil and John—had to cope with every ailment asunder the following week, even though they had Monday off.

A heatwave, a sudden deluge of summer visitors and their combined efforts to help with Ben all added to the chaos. She gazed at him now, playing in the garden of her own house. It was the last day of the school holiday and since she had no surgery until twelve she had offered to have Ben that morning whilst Marcus went to the hospital. Ben's dark head bent over the fence to stroke next door's dog.

The huge fluffy animal loped excitedly up and down and Ben's laughter drifted in through the open window. Thank God he hadn't known how ill his mother had been—or his little sister. And the baby was still not out of danger yet. Jaundice had set in as the doctors had feared and respiratory distress had slowed little Emma Jane's recovery.

'When am I going to see Mummy?' Ben called suddenly, bounding in through the door.

'Uncle Phil will be here soon. He's going to take you to the hospital.'

'Will you come, too?'

'I'd like to,' Cenna said regretfully, 'but I have to be at surgery. Now, have you got your card?'

Ben thrust into the pocket of his jeans. 'Here it is. See? "Get well, Mummy and Emma,"' he read as his small brow creased and he pointed to the now rather crumpled card they had created on the computer. 'Mummy will get better, won't she, Aunt Cenna?'

Cenna, dressed in a dark blue suit for work, paused as she lifted her case. 'Of course she will, Ben.'

'But my first mummy didn't and I don't even remember her because I was only a baby like Emma.'

Cenna's heart squeezed as she bent down beside him. 'Mummy and Emma are both going to come home,' she reassured him firmly. 'And you'll be able to help Mummy a great deal by looking after your baby sister.'

Ben stared at her with his deep brown eyes. She realised that he had associated himself as a baby with his birth mother's death and now he had the same fears for Jane.

'Listen, that sounds like Uncle Phil now,' she said quickly, and was relieved to see a beaming smile.

When Phil rang the bell, Ben ran to answer it. 'Look at my card, Uncle Phil. We made it on the computer. Shall I get in the car? Bye, Cenna!'

Phil grinned as he watched the boy bound down the path to the car. 'I rather thought that would be the case,' he said as Cenna locked the door behind her and they followed Ben. 'He seems in good spirits today.'

'I'm just a little concerned about something he said,' Cenna remarked as they watch Ben clamber in the car. 'Has he mentioned his real mother to you by any chance?'

'No. Not at all. Why?'

'He did today.'

'In what respect?'

'That he didn't recall her because he was a baby when she died—the same situation, he must think, as Emma and Jane.'

Phil frowned as they stopped at the gate. 'It might be worth mentioning that to Marcus. He was a bit worried about Ben missing Jane and that was before Emma's appearance. Obviously, the way it all happened was a shock for him.'

'Are you staying at the hospital?' Cenna asked as she glanced at her watch.

'No—just dropping Ben off. Then I'm off on my calls.

And—' he looked at her with amusement in his expressive dark eyes '—I thought I'd warn you, when you go in, you've a surgery booked until five tonight. I'll get back as soon as I can and help. Can you believe the waiting room is already bursting at its seams? Any amount of TRs, I'm afraid.'

She grinned. 'Oh, we'll cope. We have done all week.'

'And some.'

He touched her arm lightly and for a second she wondered what he was about to say, but then her heart seemed almost to stop as he grinned and murmured, 'Is there any chance of fitting in an odd hour or two together this weekend?'

She tried to think of something to say that didn't give away the fact she was recalling their kiss and how she had been on the point of desperation ever since. She tried to think of a cool and calm response that would let him know that the answer was yes.

But Cenna couldn't bring herself to say the one small word. Her lips trembled and under the wing of dark hair that fell across her face her amber eyes reflected the tall, dark man standing close to her.

'Perhaps tomorrow afternoon.' He shrugged. 'I'm on call that night through till Monday. But Marcus and Ben will be at the hospital, so it would mean we could grab just a couple of hours...'

Then she managed to clear her throat and with a casual ease that completely belied her inner panic, she murmured, 'Yes, that would be lovely.'

'Good.' Phil gave her a smile to die for, then strode around to the driver's side of his car. Below him Ben's little nose was pressed against the window and her joy was tempered by a compassion and pity that knew no bounds.

That afternoon Cenna and John Hill fought their way through an endless list of temporary residents. Many complained of the wait they were forced to endure.

Occasionally, Cenna had to admit, a thirty-minute delay could seem like three hours. However, the problems that were brought to her attention—mild sunburn from a warmer than expected Easter sun, hay fever and tummy upsets—were the run of the mill until, at almost five o'clock, a young father and his son caused an uproar in the waiting room.

'I've put them in treatment room one,' Paula, the practice nurse, said in a breathless voice as she appeared in between patients. 'The father's more distressed than the little boy, who's six. He's cut his leg—it does need stitching, I think. Could you come in and see?'

'Who's waiting?' Cenna asked as she rose from the desk.

'Don't ask.' Paula frowned.

'And is Dr Jardine still on his calls?'

'Afraid so,' Paula said. 'But the good news is that Dr Granger has just come back from the hospital and he's going to help out.'

'Wonderful,' Cenna sighed, desperate for a cup of tea to alleviate the thirst she hadn't managed to quench since she'd come on duty. But ignoring it, she followed Paula to the treatment room where pandemonium was taking place.

Patty Howard, the Saturday morning receptionist who had volunteered to come in all Easter week, was trying to pacify an irate, dark-haired young man, whose little boy was in floods of tears.

'I demand to see a doctor—now!' the young man was shouting. 'Can't you see this is an emergency?'

'A doctor is just coming. Please, calm down, Mr Barnes.' Patty was trying to settle the little boy on the treatment couch, but he was refusing to be touched. Blood was streaming from his right leg under a makeshift bandage.

'I'm Dr Lloyd,' Cenna said, and the man flew round on

his heel. Both the boy and his father were wearing shorts and T-shirts and the little boy's shorts were covered in blood.

'You took your time, didn't you?' The young man looked furious and Cenna bent down to his son, ignoring the threats that were flowing over her head. She removed the bandage despite the boy's protests, discovered his name was Simon, then lifted him up onto the treatment couch.

'Well?' demanded the father. 'It's a wonder he hasn't bled to death in the time it took him to be seen.'

'Paula, I'll need to put some sutures in here,' Cenna said calmly, ignoring the threat. 'Could you bring the trolley over, please? Patty, thank you for your help.'

The young receptionist nodded, then fled. Paula prepared and wheeled over the trolley whilst Cenna washed her hands. Glancing at the young man, Cenna asked how and where the injury had happened. In an abrupt tone of voice he told her it had taken place on the beach on some glass embedded in the sand.

'I'm going to clean the wound, and administer some lignocaine,' she explained as she went about her work, 'so if you would like to stand on the other side of Simon, we'll have this over and done in just a few moments.'

'Will it hurt?' Simon asked in a small voice as she cleaned the cut.

'You may feel a little bit of coldness, Simon, that's all. Hold Daddy's hand, if you like. And look—Paula has brought you over a book.' Cenna glanced at Mr Barnes who had shifted to the other side of the bench and appeared to have calmed down.

When the injury was clean, Cenna gave the lignocaine plenty of time as Simon opened the book and turned the pages. The book was about football which interested Simon and as she worked she heard the boy pointing to some of the large photo plates and talking to his father.

'I want to be a footballer,' Simon was saying, unaware now of the sutures Cenna was neatly inserting in his leg.

'Well, you might be one day,' his father said, glancing at Cenna as she completed the sutures.

'Which team do you support, Simon?' Cenna asked as she sprayed his leg with antibiotic and then plastic skin.

'Manchester United,' said Simon, grinning. 'They're the best team in the world. That's where we come from.'

'We're on holiday—or supposed to be,' Mr Barnes said grudgingly.

'Usually the beach is very clean,' Cenna said as she finished. 'I'm sorry you had such a nasty experience, Simon.'

'Doesn't he need a bandage?' the young man demanded as she helped Simon down from the bench.

'No, just the light dressing to stop it snagging.'

Paula was standing at the door, and as she began to lead the way out a loud voice from the waiting room demanded to be seen. Cenna was prepared for the young man to depart without thanking her and she was surprised when he said rather sheepishly, 'You've got rather a lot going on out there. Thank you for fitting us in.'

When they had gone, Annie appeared in a hurry. 'Dr Granger's not here yet, Dr Lloyd, and the phone is still ringing.'

Cenna lifted her eyes as she removed her disposable apron. 'All right, Annie, send the next one in to me.'

'Would you like a coffee first?'

'I would, but I won't.' Cenna gave a tired smile. 'I can last out until six.'

'Looks like it might be seven tonight.' Annie lifted her eyebrows as they walked into the hall. 'I'll stay on, but Paula has to go. And Patty is leaving, too.'

'Can you cope?' Cenna asked as they halted outside her room.

'I phoned my sister and asked her to keep the kids,'

Annie said. 'It's the least I can do after everyone's support at the barbecue.'

'Gosh, I haven't asked,' gasped Cenna, closing her eyes for a second. 'Was the evening successful?'

'Fantastic,' Annie replied quickly. 'At least for school funds. I just wish it had ended a bit better for everyone else. How is Dr Granger and the baby?'

'I haven't heard today,' Cenna began, then stopped as she looked along the hall and saw Phil appear. He walked towards them with his long strides and his thick dark hair lying rather untidily across his forehead. The smile on his lips made her heart jerk and she felt the strange sensation in the pit of her stomach that always alerted her to his presence.

Then Cenna saw that he wasn't alone. Helen Prior walked in his wake, her small neat figure instantly recognisable as they stopped a little distance away outside Phil's room. They were deep in conversation and Cenna walked quickly into her own room.

She hadn't realised Annie was behind her as she stood hesitantly at her desk.

Annie said quietly, 'Well, perhaps it's better than we thought, Dr Lloyd. And maybe you might get time for that coffee now.'

Cenna looked at Annie and said vaguely, 'What? Oh, you mean Dr Jardine being here?'

Annie nodded. 'I'll ask him if he'll take one straight away—or, at least, after Dr Prior has gone. And perhaps if I tell him how fraught the afternoon's been he might…er, well, you know…' Annie's voice trailed off and with a wry smile she hurried away.

Cenna sat down at her desk, her legs feeling weak. She tried to think rationally. Helen was a doctor. There was every reason for her to be here—a dozen or more. She could be speaking to Phil professionally…of course, she would be. But try as hard as could to convince herself of this, it still didn't take away the memory of Helen's expression as she'd gazed up at Phil.

She gave herself a little shake in order to clear the disturbing image from her mind. But it remained stubbornly there, causing that dreadful pain to catch in her chest. She was still trying to deal with its effects as her next patient was shown in. And it persisted until the end of the day when, unable to shake herself free from her fears, Cenna's thoughts went into overdrive.

Saturday dawned a little overcast, but it was warm and dry and as beautiful as any April day could be. Cenna showered, did a few random household chores, then took at least an hour deciding what she was going to wear for the afternoon.

Phil had suggested they visit Jane first, but Marcus said there was talk of Jane and the baby being transferred to Southampton. Phil hadn't mentioned Helen and Cenna hadn't asked him. What could she say? She would only sound like the jealous person she was in danger of becoming.

Eventually they had decided to play their precious few hours by ear. At least it hadn't decided to rain, Cenna thought as she looked at the sky through the kitchen window. And there were no patients to see, no one to complain—and the whole day stretched ahead.

With Phil in it.

The day was warm and she decided on a summer dress, a calf-length, soft, pale green one, with a tiny belt and buttons down the front that were the same colour as her amber eyes. It made her feel as though summer had arrived. And when the doorbell rang and a burst of sunshine fell through the door, it was Phil who stood there looking devastatingly handsome in light-coloured chinos and a soft pale linen shirt. His hair was immaculate, tamed and glossy, and he smelt of something that made her catch her breath in her throat.

'You look lovely,' he told her, their eyes meeting, and she smiled. Nothing would ever make her feel comfortable when she saw him, she realised. That first, violent jerk under her ribs, the feeling of light-headedness, the weak legs. Oh, yes, the symptoms were all recognisable now—now that, after their kiss, she admitted to them.

'I'm not certain I feel it.'

'Why?' He walked in and she closed the door.

Laughing, she said, 'We've been on a roll at the surgery. I wondered if it ever was going to stop this week. I fully expected something to crop up today and—'

His eyes were dark brown pebbles as he smiled. 'And stop us from meeting?'

She laughed softly. 'Something like that.'

'Well, it hasn't and it won't. And I'm not on call until six. So we've got five long hours to fill...doing anything we like.'

She heard the catch in his voice and felt her heart pound. Something told her he was feeling the same way and she swallowed, her eyes locked with his.

'Cenna?'

She stood still. They were standing in a pool of sunshine in her small lounge. The birds outside were singing, mistakenly thinking it was summer, and even the scents of summer were drifting in. She felt heady with the mixture...expectant...disorientated. And when he moved towards her, she felt as though he were looking into her soul.

'I don't want us to rush this...this whatever it is we have.' Phil reached out, took her hands. 'I want things to be...good...for us. Sometimes it feels as though we have to cram everything in—work, patients, our lives—too quickly, too fast.'

She felt that, too, but she couldn't tell him. It didn't matter. Not as long as he was here. Not as long as he was holding her hands, not as long—

'Let's go for a drive,' he said quickly, so quickly she jumped.

'Yes, that would be nice.'

'We'll have a slow afternoon. Steady down our pace. Enjoy every minute. Talk.'

Cenna was enjoying every minute of his company. She didn't have to move from the spot. Her entire world was here in this pool of sunshine. And talking—she couldn't talk, but she could listen for ever. She wanted so much of him.

Was she asking too much? Were they going too fast? Is that what he was saying? And suddenly she knew it was. It was then the thoughts of Helen returned, sweeping over her like a dark, gloomy cloud. The questions resurfaced in her mind, taunting her. The image of Helen looking up at Phil, her wide eyes and lovely face that were so like Maggie's…

A few minutes later, they were sitting in the car and the countryside was flashing past. She was content to be there alongside him, watching the way he drove, his long brown fingers curled around the wheel. His craggy profile was concentrated, the muscles in his arms and legs working automatically as he drove.

Making one final effort, she tried to dismiss Helen from her mind, exerting all her strength to concentrate on the moment and the man sitting beside her. And, most of all, to leave the ghosts behind.

CHAPTER SIX

IT WAS a day sent from heaven, a glorious, soft, sparkling afternoon that made their long walk through the New Forest like a dream. The ferns and trees were as luminously green as she had ever seen them. Splashes of burnt umber left over from autumn transfigured the patches of blue and yellow clouds of wild flowers.

There were ponies and cattle and children and long unending pathways that cut across heaths of heather. There were small thatched cafés and villages that made Cenna want to browse in each one. And when they did stop the car and walk, Phil held her hand and life felt complete.

They strolled, arms touching, fingers entwined. Drank tea, devoured scones, laughed and talked. Phil had been right, she realised. They were different people away from work. They were beginning to know each other. After almost four years of being friends and colleagues, this was something more.

Much more.

And it was terrifying. Had she ever felt this way before? she asked herself as she watched Phil's tall figure bring a tray towards them, setting it on the small café table hidden under a striped umbrella. Had she ever felt remotely like this with Mark?

But it was hard now to even recall Mark's face.

'Eat up.' He grinned as he set the tray on the table. 'And no backing out of the carrot cake. It's home-made.'

'It's enormous!' She gaped at the thick, creamy wedges. 'And we've already eaten.'

'I defy you not to,' he told her ruefully, 'since the lady

behind the counter looks as though she might take one discarded crumb as a personal insult.' He sat down and rubbed his hands together before plunging into the cake.

'In that case—' she grinned '—I'd better try to do it justice.' She slid a piece into her mouth and closed her eyes. 'Unbelievable.'

'Just like you.'

When Cenna opened her eyes, he was staring at her. She felt her face heat up and she turned her attention back to the cake. She surprised herself, devouring every morsel seconds after Phil had finished his.

'I really didn't think you'd do it,' he said as he mopped his mouth then leaned across, lifted her napkin and brushed a crumb from her lips.

She shivered, staying perfectly still. 'I'd eat a horse if I was hungry enough.'

He took his hand away slowly and, dropping the napkin on his plate, leaned muscular brown arms on the table. 'Maggie had the appetite of a bird.'

This was it, she realised, what she had been waiting for. The mention of Maggie. She had been trying to think how she would bring up the subject, deciding against every possibility. And now here it was, as easy as that.

'She was very slender,' she said, not too quickly and trying to bring to mind any detail she could recall of Phil's beautiful wife.

He nodded, his eyes slightly unfocused. 'Maggie was anorexic.'

'Anorexic?' she repeated incredulously. 'Oh, Lord, Phil, I'm sorry.'

There was a hitch in his voice when he spoke again. 'We thought we'd cracked it, but it wasn't to be. God knows, we tried hard enough.'

For a moment she stared at him. 'I had no idea.'

'No one did. That, perhaps, was the very worst part. Hiding the truth. Avoiding situations and meeting people. Meals out, of course, were a nightmare.' Cenna waited for him to continue, the grief in his eyes so palpable she felt she could touch it. 'Maggie had treatment as a teenager,' Phil went on after a pause. 'And after we married, for a while she was well. But I don't have to tell you that anorexia sufferers need specialist treatment. I wish to God now that I had tried harder.'

He stopped suddenly and the mask that had slipped down went back into place as he said, 'I don't know why I should talk about her now. Today was meant for us.' He stood then, reaching out for her hand. 'Come on. Let's have a slow stroll back to the car.'

She made no protest but what he had told her explained so much about Maggie Jardine. The fact they'd hardly ever seen her at staff functions, her acute thinness which no one had ever questioned—why should they? Models were always thin.

But now she understood Phil's reluctance to discuss Maggie. He must have loved her very much. Very deeply. And this brought her to her senses. Out of the dream she had been living in since he'd kissed her. A touch of reality, a sharp sliver of real ice had touched her soul where her love had been growing for him.

The pain in his eyes had said it all, the agony and the misery. To lose a wife in an accident was grief enough, but to have suffered for her in life was an incomprehensible pain.

And when they started to walk through the village again, hand in hand, Maggie seemed to be there, walking with them, even in the silence.

Maggie…wasn't that what she'd wanted? Cenna asked herself harshly. Hadn't she wanted Phil to open up and speak of his late wife? Even Jane had suggested she try to get him to open up.

'Five o'clock,' Phil said as they entered the deserted car park. 'I'm afraid we'll have to start back.'

At the car he opened her door and then, as she was about to get in, he took her wrist. 'Cenna…wait…'

She let herself be drawn into his arms, longing to hold him close.

'We haven't talked about the other evening…' His voice was low and soft and his dark eyes enquiring as he gazed down on her face.

'We haven't,' she agreed, 'but, then, there's no need.'

'Isn't there?' He held her gently, his face creased in puzzlement.

'Phil, I *wanted* that kiss. I don't regret it. And I'm happy…just to be doing this, spending time with you.'

He tilted her chin up towards him. 'Do you want to do it again?'

Cenna's voice was shaky as she replied. 'I think you know the answer to that.'

He nodded slowly, then bent his head to kiss her, cupping her face between his hands. She responded at once, her fingers stroking the strong nape of his neck, pushing up into the rich thickness of his hair, pulling him harder against her mouth. Her lips opened eagerly, her mouth receiving the kiss she seemed to have been waiting an eternity for.

She clung to him, her body pressed against his, absorbing his strength and heat. Wanting, too, the inner part of him that he had only just begun to reveal. She felt the hot urgency of his tongue against her lips and she opened up to him as he searched the sweetness of her mouth.

As his kiss deepened and his arms brought her closer, Cenna made herself a promise. She wouldn't give up. She would fight Maggie if she had to. And when they finally broke apart and she slid shakily into the car, she made the

vow again. She would fight for him. Oh, yes…she would
fight.

With all her heart.

The reason, Cenna discovered, that Helen had visited the
surgery again last week had been down to Phil. On the
journey home that Saturday he explained that Helen had
agreed to help them out whilst Jane was away. She had
volunteered to take two days of surgery a week for the next
month, which, Phil remarked, he thought was very good of
her in view of her commitments with her own practice in
Stockton.

So the following week the pressure eased somewhat, despite another influx of temporary residents. Helen's small
figure graced the surgery on Tuesdays and Thursdays and
her bubbly presence became a familiar feature during cof-
fee-breaks.

The news from Marcus was that baby Emma and Jane
had remained at the cottage hospital. Jane didn't want
Marcus to have to travel to Southampton and she'd opposed
the move rigorously.

On Tuesday evening Cenna left a card and parcel at the
hospital. Inside was the smallest pink towelling suit she
could find, with white embroidered daisies, and by Friday
Marcus had told her that Jane was delighted.

'If it's OK, I'll call in to see her at the weekend,' Cenna
said to Marcus as they stood in the office.

'She'd love it.' Marcus looked tired, she thought.

'Would there be room for another one to tag along?' Phil
asked, and crooked an eyebrow.

'Of course.' Marcus shrugged. 'She'll want to catch up
on all the news.'

Phil chuckled. 'One thing I'm not going to do is talk
shop.'

Cenna smiled wryly. 'No, you'll be talking babies.'

'I'd better clue up on the subject.' Phil grinned, throwing her a quick glance. 'What time is visiting on Sunday?'

'Two until five,' Marcus replied, 'and you won't get in before. The baby unit is like Fort Knox.'

'John's on weekend call,' Phil said afterwards as they walked to their rooms. 'So, what if I take you for a meal after the hospital visit?'

She looked up at him and smiled. 'Yes—I'd like that.'

'I'd suggest the Summerville—' Phil grinned '—if I didn't know better.'

'I'm down with a bug,' John said groggily over the phone early on Saturday morning. 'Temperature, nausea, no legs. Started last night. This morning I can barely put one foot in front of another.'

'Stay in bed,' Cenna advised as she sat up. The ringing of the phone had awoken her.

'I'm supposed to be on duty.'

'Don't worry. We'll cope.'

'At a time like this—'

'John, stop worrying. Climb back into bed and stay there till you feel better.'

'Thanks, Cenna. Damn virus!'

She lifted herself wearily from bed, stretched and pushed her hair from her eyes. After she had put on her dressing-gown and made a cup of tea, she rang Marcus, explaining.

'I'll do the weekend,' she told him, knowing that her chance of seeing Phil on Sunday was now out of the window. Marcus had Ben to cope with and that only left Phil whose own on-call duty was Monday night. 'You're still OK to take this morning's surgery?'

'Yes,' Marcus agreed. 'And thanks.'

'I don't know now if I'll be able to get in to see Jane. But I'll try.'

Cenna went back upstairs, showered and dressed. She

left ringing Phil until she'd had breakfast. And when she did, she tried not to sound disappointed.

'Another time,' he told her.

But she wasn't certain whether there was just a hint of relief in his voice.

Baby Emma was gorgeous.

She was enclosed in a thermostatically controlled cabinet designed to maintain her body temperature and supply oxygen when necessary. She looked lost in the hospital nappy but she wore a soft spotted top rolled back to expose her small tummy. She had a blonde tuft of hair and her skin colour was improving by the day as she recovered from the jaundice.

Cenna stood with Jane in the over-warm hospital hallway as they looked through the glass at Emma, fast asleep. It was half past six on Sunday and Cenna had been uncertain whether or not the staff would admit her, going on Marcus's warning. But luckily the ward wasn't busy and Sister had made an exception when Cenna had explained she was on call and might have to dash away any minute.

They had been talking for the best part of a quarter of an hour and Cenna was praying her pager didn't go off. The afternoon had seen both the mobile phone and pager in almost constant action and she and Jane had crammed into their fifteen minutes as much news as they could, knowing any minute they may be disturbed.

'Have you any idea when you'll be home?' Cenna asked Jane, whose blue eyes were tired and the small lines that ran out from them like tiny rivers spoke of the anxiety that she still felt for the baby.

'Not yet. Not until the feeding is established. At the moment I'm trying combination feeding, so that she has as much as possible by breast or bottle and the tube supplies the rest.'

'Is she sucking now?' Cenna asked curiously as she gazed at the tiny form of Emma Jane Granger asleep in her cabinet.

'With persuasion,' Jane sighed. 'I gently stroke her cheek then the centre of her lip, and she tries to open her mouth, but we've been hampered by apnoea.'

'Oh, that's miserable,' Cenna murmured sympathetically.

'I sympathise with any mother,' Jane said with a frown, 'whose baby has suffered from respiratory distress. When a baby stops breathing even for a few seconds it's quite terrifying. Most babies start breathing again after a gentle tap or two but in that time your heart stands still.'

Cenna didn't know how she herself would react in such a situation. A new life was an overwhelming responsibility. Any doctor was aware of the possibilities. The fact that oxygen via a face mask could be given in the worst of scenarios—or a tube inserted into the windpipe—was of no comfort at all.

'Are you feeling stronger?' Cenna asked, turning her attention to Jane.

Jane was wearing a light cotton smock and had pulled her blonde hair back into a band. She looked very pale, but she smiled as she met Cenna's eyes. 'I'm feeling much better—really.'

'You had us worried for a while,' Cenna admitted softly. 'Especially poor Marcus.'

'He's convinced it happened because I'd been rushing around and the blood pressure shot up.'

'And he's probably right,' Cenna said firmly, only to be poked in the ribs.

'Don't you start.' Jane grinned. 'He lectures me every day about resting when I come home.'

'For your own good,' Cenna pointed out, 'and the baby's. I can't think how, at the barbecue, I didn't notice that you weren't well.'

'I didn't want to admit it myself,' Jane said as they walked over to the easy chairs and sat down. 'Most of all, I didn't want to upset Ben. This has all been so...so dramatic for him, poor little fellow.'

'When you're feeling better and Emma's feeding,' Cenna suggested, 'why don't you slip out, collect him from school and take him home? Try to turn the whole hospital episode around. I'm sure Sister and the staff will cope with Emma whilst you're away, if it's not for too long.'

Jane looked suddenly brighter. 'Yes, that's a wonderful idea. I'll mention it to Marcus.' She paused, then looked at Cenna wryly. 'Stop me from talking about babies all the time. What's happened at the surgery? Marcus tells me Helen Prior from the Stockton practice is helping out.'

Relieved that her suggestion had gone down well, Cenna nodded slowly. 'I don't know her very well and we've only really spoken this week. I met her a couple of times some years back but only very briefly.'

'Did Phil explain why they were at the Summerville together?' Jane asked curiously.

'Yes. He said that he'd made plans to travel to Oxford to see Maggie's parents and at the last minute they were cancelled.'

'And then Helen made her appearance?' Jane sighed.

As Cenna looked at Jane she saw a smile lifting her lips, and it wasn't long before they were both giggling.

'Oh, it's so good to laugh again,' Jane said breathlessly as she leaned back in the chair. But after a while she sniffed and murmured, 'Cenna...I do miss home.'

Cenna laid a hand on her friend's arm. 'It won't be long now.'

'I'd go through it all again for Emma, but time drags being away from Ben and Marcus. Especially Ben. I do worry over him.' She turned and, blinking misty eyes, whispered, 'He is...all right, isn't he?'

'Of course he is.' Cenna tried to reassure Jane, but felt a guilty pang as she did so as she thought of what Ben had told her. 'Missing you, but delighted to have a baby sister.' She touched Jane's arm. 'Now I'm going so that you can have some rest. I'll call again next week, possibly with Phil.'

'Does that mean what I think it means?'

Cenna felt her cheeks redden.

'Don't answer that,' Jane said as she stood up. 'I'll use my imagination. After all, that's all I've got to do all day.'

They parted on laughter, but as Cenna left the hospital she felt anxious for Jane. They weren't out of the woods yet with baby Emma and there was Ben's reaction to deal with when Jane returned home. Suddenly the thought of her own home was overwhelmingly attractive and Cenna quickly jumped into the car. But her hopes of returning home were dashed as the mobile phone demanded her attention. A few minutes later she was driving in the opposite direction.

The following Tuesday, John Hill returned to work, with sniffs and snuffles but, on the whole, better. By Thursday, Cenna had visited Jane again, though not with Phil who had gone to see her on another day because of pressure of work. They were both relieved to find mother and baby doing well, despite small feeding setbacks.

Helen was achieving two full surgeries a week. Cenna had chatted to her in the staffroom, finding her company surprisingly easy. Helen had a number of tales to tell about life with her two husbands from whom she was divorced, and Cenna had to admit she brightened up the atmosphere which had grown rather tense since Jane's departure.

It was on the Tuesday afternoon of the following week that Homer Pomeroy limped into Cenna's room. He sat down on the chair by her desk with a monumental sigh.

Had it not been for his hangdog expression, Cenna would have been prepared for his usual dismissive comments about his health. But something alerted her to the fact that his attitude had changed and she waited for him to speak.

After a few moments he gathered himself. 'You're absolutely right,' he said as he thrust out his chin. 'It's gout. And, of course, you've been telling me for months.'

She glanced at his records and frowned. 'A little longer than that, actually. Almost two years.'

'I don't doubt it,' Homer agreed reluctantly. 'But it's taken me until now to realise I've been causing everyone a good deal of consternation. You see...' he looked quickly from side to side '...I've had a brush with the law. I expect you read all about it in the newspapers. Luckily I got off with a caution.'

'If you really are going to take better care of your health, then perhaps it was all worth it,' Cenna remarked tactfully.

He smiled wryly. 'Good way to look at it, I suppose.'

'So how can I help you today?'

Homer paused. 'I suppose it's no use asking you for one of those jabs, is it?'

'It is—if one is necessary. Have I your word that you'll take your medication?'

Homer nodded solemnly. 'Without a doubt.'

'The level of uric acid in the test we did was very high,' Cenna continued, unwilling this time to allow Homer off the hook. 'Therefore your medication must be taken for life and not stopped. And you must change your diet and—'

'Alcohol consumption,' Homer supplied for her, looking hangdog once again. 'Yes, I realise that. I'm going to jump on the wagon.'

'There are organisations to help,' Cenna pointed out, softening her tone as it really did seem as though Homer was trying.

'Thanks all the same, but I've had an ultimatum. Gun at the head, so to speak. Enough incentive to behave myself.'

Cenna crooked an eyebrow. 'An ultimatum?'

Homer nodded. 'Mrs V. Gave her notice in after the…er…pub debacle.'

'Mrs V.—your housekeeper?'

'Been with me years. Salt of the earth. Don't care to lose her. Made a promise now to be a good boy.'

'I see. Well, let's see what can be done today.' Cenna allowed herself a small smile as she rose and Homer followed her into the treatment room. As he removed the slipper that covered an ugly swollen toe and hoisted himself up onto the couch, he began to tell her about his engagement—or rather the break-up of it when he'd become so jealous of one of his fiancée's admirers that he'd tried to hit him.

'Missed the swine by yards and fell flat on my backside,' Homer admitted as he lay there.

Cenna knew that Homer's days were numbered in the fighting department, for as she touched the red, swollen and extremely tender leg Homer grimaced in pain.

'I'm afraid there's swelling around your ankle and big toe now,' Cenna said with a sigh as she examined the leg. 'Have you had much pain?'

Homer nodded. 'A couple of days after your visit it started. The pain was, I have to admit, pretty excruciating.'

'And it lasted at that intensity for a day or more?'

'I couldn't stand on it at all yesterday,' Homer admitted. 'And I haven't been able to tolerate the pressure of the bedclothes, or socks or shoes.' He glanced at her hopefully. 'Do you think it's just a one-off by any chance?'

Cenna looked her patient in the eye. 'You've had an acute attack in your toe and lower leg, where the pain reaches a high level for twenty-four or even thirty-six hours. You may never have another attack but, then, your knee is still badly affected and a second attack could occur. I'll put you straight onto a large dose of a nonsteroidal antiinflammatory drug and the inflammation should subside. Abstain from alcohol and, as I've suggested before, avoid foods high in purine. Liver, offal, poultry and pulses are the worst offenders.'

Homer awkwardly sat up and lowered his feet to the floor. When he had rolled down his trouser leg and put on his slipper, he sighed. 'What an old wreck I am. Ready for the scrapheap almost.'

'Not if you take care of yourself,' Cenna remarked as they returned to her desk.

She gave him his prescription, accompanied by one last lecture about his diet and fluid consumption, and off he went with many assurances to change. She had no idea whether he would keep them, but she hoped he would. Without a change in lifestyle, Homer Pomeroy would become a very sick man.

It was as she was closing the door, her mind still on Homer and his troubles, that Phil's voice filtered down the hall and she opened the door again.

'Oh, dear.' He frowned as he hurried towards her. 'Homer looks in a bad way.'

'You saw him?'

'We passed in Reception, though I think he tried to avoid me.'

Cenna sighed. 'With reason. The gout has spread.'

'Not a surprise, by any means,' Phil said, one eyebrow quirked.

'No, but he's promised to stop drinking and change his diet.'

'Do you believe him?'

Cenna grinned. 'If his housekeeper has anything to do with his good intentions, yes.'

Phil gave her a wry look. 'And what if his long lost love arrives back on the scene?'

'Don't even think about it,' Cenna said in horror.

'So you agree she isn't a very good influence?'

Cenna pushed the dark hair from her eyes and leaned casually against the doorframe, though she didn't feel very casual as she looked up into Phil's teasing brown eyes. 'We could all say that about someone in our lives,' she remarked dryly.

He raised one arm and leaned it against the doorframe above her. 'Don't tempt me...'

'To what?' she mumbled, her heart racing.

'To being the worst influence in yours and suggesting we both try to get away early on Friday and go for a drink.'

'Abandon my patients?' Cenna tried to make a joke of it whilst her heart beat a tattoo in her chest.

He nodded slowly. 'And then I'll cook you something to eat—if you like. At home.'

She couldn't believe he had just said that... Had she heard right? She lifted herself up from her leaning position and swallowed. 'Home?' she repeated lamely. 'Do you mean mine or yours?'

'Either.' He grinned, appearing to savour her discomfort. 'But preferably mine, since I know my way around my own kitchen and not yours.' Phil tilted his head sideways and she swallowed again.

'Yes...well, fine,' she gabbled, faintly aware that Helen was walking towards them and had an expression on her face that could be defined as either shocked or stunned— but Cenna thought the latter was probably accurate.

CHAPTER SEVEN

CENNA wanted it, yet she dreaded it—seeing the house again. Phil's house. She corrected herself as she felt a tinge of guilt—Phil's and Maggie's house. It had been a long time since she'd set foot in it, the last time shortly after the funeral. It had been a dreadful Christmas. The tragedy had hung like a pall over the surgery. She'd driven up here to ask Phil if there was anything she could do. She'd known the answer before she'd arrived, but she'd had to try.

He'd taken a week off—just a week. And he'd looked dreadful. He'd lost weight and had had trouble with his memory. Everyone had guessed it had been the shock and had begged him to rest. He'd refused—bar for the week. And though the skiing accident had happened in November, it had been nearer Christmas by the time Maggie had been brought home and the arrangements made for the funeral.

Probably the worst time of the year.

Cenna let her eyes linger on the shimmering sweep of sea to their left and the cliff road leading to the small pub sheltering under green sycamores. Beyond this, the next turn on the left and a winding lane brought the visitor to a narrow track only really accessible by a single vehicle.

'So, a drink first and then home?' Phil turned the Mercedes into the pub car park and pulled up under the trees. 'We can sit outside if you like—it's still warm.'

'We could just have a drink,' she floundered. 'It's been a busy Friday—'

'No, not just a drink,' he said, his hand resting on the car door. 'I want you to come home.'

Cenna looked into Phil's dark eyes, trying not to panic.

Was he being polite? Was he already regretting inviting her home? She wanted to give him the option to change his mind, yet she clung to every little hope.

And hope flared again as he turned and slid his arm along the back of the seat. Hope that sent the air out of her lungs in a whoosh as he smiled and took her hand, a quizzical expression on his face. 'Unless you're trying to tell me you'd prefer not to go on from here.'

'No, of course not,' she answered quickly. 'I just don't want you to think you have to do this—'

'I'm doing nothing I don't want to do.' His smile faded and his hand came up and cupped her jaw. 'We could sit here all evening, discussing the pros and cons of whether this is right.'

She took a breath and nodded. 'We could...'

'Or we could just go for it. Forget about the rules and enjoy ourselves.' A smile touched his lips. 'And, frankly, I was hoping it was the latter.'

With her heart pounding she wondered what rules he was referring to. But she managed weakly, 'Me, too.'

They got out of the car and walked hand in hand under the rose archway. The soft murmur of voices from the garden was enough to tell them it was fairly busy in the pub, so they occupied the nearest seat, a wooden bench and table by a pond.

The fronds of palms shimmered in the warm evening air and an early vine that hung over the fence shed a fragile scent. One bat swooped, followed by another and another, disappearing like tiny elves into the thatch.

Phil went into the pub to buy the drinks and she pulled her sweater around her shoulders. Faint strains of classical music floated out from the bar and she leaned back on the bench, absorbing the night and the music as the events of the day tumbled through her mind erratically. A busy morning surgery, the antenatal clinic this afternoon and her final surgery at four. Her face crimsoned as she sat there recalling the swiftness with which she had concluded it, rushing up to the cloakroom to change her clothes.

Luckily, there had been just two late emergencies, patients wanting repeat prescriptions only. She'd had her clothes prepared in her gym bag, an uncrushable summer dress in a soft pale blue and sandals to match, praying none of the girls would remark on her swift change from suit to casual as she left by the back way.

She'd pinned up her dark hair, applied a dab of moisturiser to her nose, a gentle pale pink shadow of lipstick. And then she'd fled, heart in mouth. A new receptionist had been on duty and Annie had been busy locking up. So she'd escaped easily, driving her car home where Phil had been waiting outside her house in the Mercedes.

It had all felt rather Machiavellian, but if she'd left her car in the surgery car park there would have been speculation…

Now she persuaded her tense body to breathe slowly, unclench fingers and recall some yoga technique to relax. She'd ordered a white wine and Phil brought her back a glass that was deliciously chilled and a shandy for himself.

He sat beside her, stretching out, his dark suit suddenly looking restrictive as he hauled off his jacket and thrust it over the seat. 'So…' he sighed, stretching out beside her, his long body curled, one foot propped up on his knee. 'We made it.'

Cenna laughed, despite the weirdest of sensations running around her tummy. 'Yes, but I could have driven here—met you at the pub. I don't know why we didn't do it that way.'

'Because I wanted you to relax,' he told her simply. 'The track that leads to my house,' he'd insisted yesterday when they'd finalised plans, 'is a nightmare in the dark. No lighting at all. Leave your car at home and I'll drive.'

So she'd agreed. And here they were.

'It's nice,' she admitted honestly, 'to be pampered.'

She wanted to tell Phil the feel of his warm body beside her was special enough. That her heart was racing so that it actually hurt to breathe. That her legs felt completely unreal, even her toes tingling.

But, of course, she didn't.

She didn't tell him either that it was wonderful to think of a whole evening ahead—uninterrupted.

'Tell me about Mark,' he said suddenly, catching her off guard. All her emotions went into overdrive again. She swallowed, tried to think of an excuse not to talk about Mark, then knew she was trapped.

'We knew each other in our teens,' she said, and stopped, breathing hard as his fingers dropped casually from the back of the bench and brushed the bare skin of her arm. 'Our mothers were friends. It was a small town…not a lot going on. We were about the same age, liked each other reasonably well so we dated. Mark always wanted to be a lawyer, I always wanted to be a doctor. At first we had a lot in common. Or so we thought.'

'What happened to change that?' His voice was low, the touch of his fingers mesmerising.

'Our careers, I think. We were ambitious—wanted to move from the Midlands, wanted all the things we thought would bring happiness…'

'And…?' he prompted as she paused.

'And then, as time went on…' She trapped her lip under her teeth, biting down to keep her voice level. 'We made friends in other circles—had other agendas—other social commitments.'

'And because of that you broke up?'

'Not directly. Something else happened.' Cenna looked down, feeling him close against her yet not wanting to meet his eyes. She hadn't wanted to talk about this. 'Mark met someone,' she said very softly. Phil leaned forward to hear her. 'It was nothing serious, he said. And I might have believed him if he'd told me about it, but he didn't. I found out—and it was the way I found out that hurt. From some-one else—a little harmless gossip.' She shrugged. 'You can guess the rest.'

'I don't have to guess,' he said, and she looked at him. 'Remember? I saw you at the Summerville.'

'That was a mistake.'

'I don't think he thought it was.'

She shook her head, blinking rapidly. 'It was over a long time before he moved south. I just happened to be here, someone he'd known from the past…'

'Someone *special* he'd known. And…' He stopped, his voice lowering as he went on rather raggedly, 'I can sym-pathise entirely. You're a very beautiful woman, Cenna. Mark made a mistake on a very grand scale and no doubt he regrets it.'

She glanced up, shocked at his words, her eyes searching his as they sat there, trapped in the moment, until suddenly the music changed its beat and a rapid pounding shook the peace of the garden.

'I think it's time to go,' he said softly, and she nodded. They stood and he pulled her sweater around her, the touch of his fingers sending a flood of goose-bumps over her skin. Hand in hand they left the garden, their drinks half-finished, and a short while later the Mercedes was nosing its way down the narrow lane that led towards Phil's home.

His house was a large, red-brick property with white painted gables, the gravel drive fringed by neat lawns. Phil parked the Mercedes and opened the white-painted Georgian door, showing Cenna into the spacious hall. She recalled last time she had come here shortly after the fu-neral. Phil had shown her into his study—an untidy, com-fortable room that had felt warm and restful.

But on this occasion he took her through to the lounge, a pleasant room, with no lack of comfortable furnishings and wide windows at one end leading out onto the lawn. But even so Cenna sensed a certain lack of warmth, despite the books, paperwork and magazines that littered the tables and chairs.

'Make yourself at home,' Phil told her as he flung his coat on the back of the long, white sofa. 'Forgive the clutter. I had to dash out this morning. I'm slightly behind.' He took her hand and led her through to the kitchen. Before they went in, he held a hand over her eyes. 'Ready?' he asked teasingly.

'Is it that bad?'

'I want to soften the blow.' He chuckled. 'You may never be the same woman again.'

'I'll take the risk.'

He sighed and lowered his hand. Surprisingly Cenna saw nothing that alarmed her, just the simple evidence of a man living on his own and struggling to come to terms with housework. Vegetables scattered on worktops, knives, spoons and forks dotted between. Pots and pans in untidy heaps, a chef's apron tossed over a stool, a dozen reminders stuck on the fridge.

A recipe book propped open, two long-stemmed glasses on a tray, napkins unthreaded through rings, a coffee-percolator with dregs, small piles of hurriedly rinsed china—above the dishwasher.

'OK,' Phil muttered, swinging into action. 'Where to start…'

'What did you have in mind?' Cenna walked to the worktop and peered at the book.

'Any one of those.' Phil jabbed a finger. 'Pasta, um, in sauce and, um, salad.' He assembled the ingredients he had bought, shuffling them about on the worktop. A garlic clove bounced onto the floor and she bent to pick it up.

He bent, too, and they almost cracked heads.

'Sorry—'

'Oh, sorry—'

Then suddenly they were in each other's arms and his mouth found hers, parting her lips with the same hunger they had shared before, only this time it was clear he wanted her too much to let her go.

And she didn't want him to let her go. She wanted no food, nothing now, just the bliss of his arms around her and the feel of his mouth, his tongue weaving its way into the sweet, waiting corners of her mouth. She could feel his strong fingers around her, the pressure of his hands bringing her fiercely towards him. Clumsily they staggered upwards.

Her breath left her lungs as she forced herself to open her eyes. She wanted to know if this was happening, if this was really true. She wanted to believe what seemed like a dream. A moan rose in her mouth as she gulped, his eyes on fire as she gazed into them.

Then he eased her against the worktop and drew his hands down her bare arms, breathless and flushed. She caught a breath and let it go. She knew she was trembling, every part of her vulnerable to him. His solid frame pressed against her and his hands came to rest on her back, easing her towards him, fingers trickling down her spine.

He breathed her name before he kissed her again and her hands were roving over his chest, pushing up to his shoulders and then into his hair. She felt the heavy beat of his heart and her own answering as she leaned into him.

He gave another moan, a look of longing on his face. 'Cenna, it's not too late to change your mind.'

'We said that before,' she reminded him. 'And you know the answer.'

He drew her harder into his arms, his arousal as intense as hers. He kissed her again, this time slowly, pacing him-

self with a measure of control that told her they had all
night before them. Then took her hand and led her upstairs.

Cenna felt Phil's fingers tug the dress from her shoulders
and she trembled with the awareness of his touch. Though
he hadn't switched on the light, the room was aglow with
the moon, a full, silver globe in the sky unhidden by cloud.

She knew it was a large and luxurious room, though she
had never been in it before. The carpet beneath her feet felt
like thick moss, springy and warm, and the long windows
shed moonlight over the king-size bed.

Was this the bed Maggie had shared with Phil? Was this
the room in which they'd slept, talked and made love in?
Were they Maggie's things still on the dressing-table?

The light provided no clear view of the room, just shapes
and shadows. His hand curved gently over her bare shoulder and her eyes shut, blocking out the taunting thoughts
of Maggie.

Her dress fell to the floor and she knew that he was
staring at her in the moonlight. 'You're lovely,' he whispered raggedly, 'so lovely.'

She wanted to be lovely for him, but self-consciousness
suddenly intruded and in the darkness her cheeks flamed.
She wasn't a bit like Maggie, nowhere near the statuesque
beauty or the ethereal thinness. She had breasts—full and
womanly—and she had never supposed that she might want
not to have them. But now, just for an instant, she envied
the boyish figure that had captivated Phil, the willowy
beauty that he must have loved so much.

Then his hands reached round her and unclipped the
white, lacy bra and let it drop. Her breasts spilled out and
almost involuntarily her hands moved upward. But he held
them and instead, unable to take his eyes from her, guided
her fingers towards him.

Hands trembling, she slid off his shirt and surprisingly

he groaned, a small aching sound in the back of his throat that caused her to hesitate.

'Don't stop,' he said, recovering himself. 'It's been…a long while.' His words somehow reassured her and her fingers grasped in delight the tight curls of hair that she guessed would be scattered across his chest. As she also knew that as her fingers travelled further, she wouldn't find anything, but lean, tough muscle beneath.

'For me, too,' she whispered, a catch in her voice.

He tipped up her chin, his hand sliding into her hair. Drawing out the clip, it fell heavily onto her shoulders in dark waves, the moonlight silvering the strands of chestnut.

'So beautiful,' he said, and let it fall through his fingers, mesmerised by its texture. 'So rich and thick.'

Cenna brought her eyes up to meet his and in their glimmering reflection saw a desire that touched her heart. She quelled the voice inside that shouted of Maggie's beauty, her short raven-coloured crop that had made her look even more wistful, her long fawn-like limbs and painfully angular shoulders. No, she wasn't like Maggie—or Helen. Quite the opposite, in fact. But for once she didn't care.

What she saw in Phil's eyes told her that it didn't matter. That what he saw pleased him, excited him, and he drew her hands down. Her eyes wide and her breathing ragged, she unbuckled his belt and he kicked his trousers away. Shoes and socks shed, he drew her down on the bed as tension dried her mouth and roughened his movements.

Her breathing halted for a moment as he muttered, 'Protection…damn it.' And reached out to the side, yanking open a drawer.

She hadn't even considered it, fool that she was. She hadn't because she hadn't really believed this would happen, that she would ever be making love with him. Gently, she reached out, too, laying her own arm across his, and for a moment they lay still.

His eyes met hers and even in the darkness they blazed.

'Wait,' she said, surprising herself. 'Hold me first.'

He rolled against her, dragging her into his arms, muttering something, but she didn't hear the words. Her heart was pounding too heavily.

Then the tension drained as they held one another, her body shivering, and he pulled the quilt over them. He stroked her hair as they lay there, then trailed his fingers down and they paused on her arm.

She tipped up her head and slowly he leaned towards her, kissing her gently, as though starting all over again. Her hand slid over his hip, hard and masculine, and his palm reached hers, quivering over the elastic of her briefs. Now they had found pace, the panic over, the delight just beginning, and it was with strong and confident arms that he drew her against him and gently eased her panties over her legs, reaching up to explore the soft femininity of her naked hips.

'Cenna...' He breathed her name but no more and she slid against him, burning up now, the tension building again, dragging a shuddering sigh from her throat as his hand eased between her legs. He groaned, warning her he was close, and she nodded, gulping back the air into her chest.

Caressing the soft skin of her inner thigh, she gasped at his touch, alight with pleasure. Her movements mirrored his, though his masculine form provided almost too much pleasure to enjoy all at once.

He kissed her, and they paused, learning slowly how the rhythm worked best, knowing there would be no control when it came. Knowing they would have to let go, afraid that one of them wouldn't be there...

But the fear was unfounded. Their passion ignited, their bodies entwined as she arched for his entry. He moved above her, tenderly, exploringly, until the moment when his eyes met hers and he tensed.

'Have you…?' she whispered, her voice drowned by need.

He nodded and she knew they were safe as desire returned with a need that was almost a pain. She called out and he responded, moving at her pace, arching with her, to a harder, faster motion, satisfying her every need. When it came, it was perfect. Blood pounded in her ears until the noise filled her whole body like a tidal wave, consuming her.

She cried out again and this time he was with her, all the way. They moved as one, curled, arched, stretched to their limit and, finally exhausted, sank back into the folds of the bed, his arm trapped beneath her.

And even then it hadn't finished. His tongue slicked her damp cheek and nibbled at her ear with a tenderness that made her want to cry. He held her in his arms, moving the wet hair from her forehead and kissing it.

'I don't know what to say,' he breathed as he held her. 'Except that it was wonderful.'

'For me, too,' she answered him softly. Then silently, to herself, she said the words that she had been afraid to say out loud. Three little words that she couldn't repeat to him, despite the overpowering urge inside her to say them.

If he had wanted to say them he would have.

But he hadn't.

And she couldn't expect him to. They had made love—once. They had only just stopped being doctors and become lovers. She didn't even know the colour of his bedroom walls.

The ridiculous thoughts urged on tears that were very close. He'd made no promises, said nothing, except once—that they were going too fast, that day in the forest. He'd wanted to slow down. And that was when she'd thought of Helen, so much a replica of Maggie.

It was then that the glint of a photo frame caught her eyes. Over his shoulder as he held her. She could see the photo and her heart gave a sudden jolt. Maggie stared out, her dark, exotic looks making her the outstanding beauty she was. Something in Maggie's expression reminded her of Helen—the way she tilted her head very slightly and the quizzical look in the dark, mysterious eyes.

Fear suddenly filled Cenna and she clung to Phil. It took all her resolve to remind herself that she was living only for the present and not for the past. And that this interlude in their lives was filling all her needs and satisfying her desires. With that thought came a measure of relief and she sank back against the pillow with a soft sigh.

He didn't take her home that night.

They woke up when it was still dark, curled into each other. Taking her in his arms, they made love again. It was an incredible act. Sleep had only heightened their desire and this time they discovered new places to kiss and lick and caress. She thought they might go on for ever until their need arose so strongly that that it was impossible to stay the moment.

When it was over, they sank down again, murmuring sighs, not words, placing small, innocent kisses on shoulders and lips, their bodies curling automatically in slumber.

They woke at seven when light filled the room. Cenna sat up with a fright, thinking she had Saturday morning surgery. But Phil pulled her down again and wrapped his arms around her. 'It's John's duty—remember?'

'I can't think,' she mumbled, praying her brain would function. 'Who's at the surgery?'

'Marcus,' said Phil gruffly as he grinned, drawing her

against him. 'Now, come here and stop trying to think of excuses to leave.'

'I'm not,' she protested. 'I could stay here all day.' Reality came crashing back as inadvertently she turned her head and saw the photo beside the bed.

Phil caught her stare and, easing himself up beside her, whispered, 'Maggie and her parents—just after our wedding.'

'She was very beautiful, Phil.'

He turned slowly and nodded as he stared at the photo. 'Yes, she was.'

Her heart seemed to flutter inside her chest and, almost as though he'd heard it, he took her in his arms and buried his face in her hair. 'It was too young to die,' he groaned, his words lost in a throaty rasp. 'Far too young for anyone to die...'

Cenna swallowed, holding his dark head against her chest. The moment seemed long and unending, his breathing hard as he held her against him. Then all at once he started kissing her hard and fiercely.

She had no strength left to fight her desire. She wanted him so much. Somewhere in her brain she calculated that Friday night's ritual shop hadn't been done and the fridge at home would remain empty. That her usual Saturday morning jog would be missed by her neighbours. The pint of milk on her doorstop would remain untouched. And that neither Maggie nor Helen were important at this moment...

By nine they were ravenous. Phil shot to the bathroom and returned in a dark blue towelling robe and waggling a toothbrush at her. 'It's new—for emergencies,' he clarified, grinning. Then he commanded her to stay in bed and he'd bring up a tray.

'Toast and eggs,' he promised. 'I'll make up for last night and spoil you.'

When he'd gone downstairs, Cenna felt restless. And there was the photo, staring at her from his side of the bed. It was tiny, the kind of photo you'd keep as a discreet reminder. Not something flashy.

She struggled towards it, her heart racing as she peered at the three figures standing with their arms linked. Propping herself up on one elbow, she reached out and lifted it, knowing at once as she brought it nearer. A tall, lean, grey-headed man with Maggie's dark eyes and generous mouth and a slender woman resembling her daughter.

A happy family once...

She returned the photo to the bedside table and gazed around the room, half seeking evidence of Maggie, half hoping she wouldn't find it. Fitted wardrobes, light-coloured drapes and vertical blinds. A light-coloured carpet. One set of plain, masculine drawers.

She went to the bathroom and used the new toothbrush. Then she found another towelling robe behind the door. It was black and crumpled and didn't feel like a woman's— it was too big. Then fleetingly she had a mental picture of Helen and tortured herself with an image that was totally insane. One glance around the shelves told her only a man bathed and shaved here.

She rinsed her hands and face, brushed her hair.

Curiosity made her venture into the hall. Four doors to the right, banisters the left. She peeked. Two of the rooms were bedrooms and two cupboards. A door at the end of the hall was a loo.

She found Phil downstairs in the kitchen, burning toast. 'You're supposed to be in bed,' he told her.

'I got lonely.'

'Blast. I've lost count on the eggs. I like mine soft. What about you?'

'Soft,' she agreed, tipping the timer.

'They're just boiling...'

'Three minutes.' She grinned, salvaging them in time.

'Hope you like crisp soldiers.' He buttered piles of toast noisily, heaping them onto plates.

'The crisper the better.' She stood behind him and wound her arms around his middle. He smelt of splash-on after-shave—and burnt toast.

'You'd better stop doing that or you'll never get anything to eat.'

She giggled. 'Is that a threat or a promise?'

'Both,' he threatened her as he finished the tray. 'Have I forgotten anything?'

'We can always come back for seconds.'

He pulled her towards him, kissing the tip of her nose. 'You really are a little glutton. I don't know why I've not noticed before.'

'Possibly because I've never slept here before.'

His dark eyes teased her. 'Does that mean to say I'm going to have to feed you like this each time?'

Her smile was hesitant. 'If there *is* going to be a next time…'

'You don't deserve an answer,' he told her shortly, then demanded she return to bed.

CHAPTER EIGHT

PHIL returned Cenna home late that evening—she was on call the following day. Her small house seemed oddly empty after he had gone. She lay for ages in a hot bath before mooching around the kitchen and making herself a sandwich at almost midnight.

She stood the pint of milk on the doorstep in her kitchen on the worktop and gazed at it as she ate. It made her smile. When she eventually emptied the milk she kept the bottle. Crazy, she knew, but she stuck a rose in it from the garden.

Phil phoned her on Sunday morning.

'Sleep well?' he asked.

'No. I think I was past sleep.'

'Me, too.'

She thought about asking him round but she knew it wasn't sensible, even though there had been only two calls out and neither the mild allergy attack nor tummy upset had been serious.

They talked for longer than either of them had intended and when she rang off she resisted the urge to lift the phone again and ask him round for a coffee, knowing they both needed sleep.

The following day at surgery she had no idea what she was going to say when she saw him. But she needn't have worried. It was chaos when she walked in.

'We had to fit five in before nine,' Annie explained breathlessly. 'Four children and a pensioner with angina.'

'Who took them?' Cenna queried as she entered the office behind Reception.

'I did,' Phil said, and she swivelled around to find him

grinning at her from behind the office desk. 'No problems that I couldn't fix—one tonsillitis, two earaches and a tetanus. The older guy was OK—couldn't find his spray and panicked. And, er…good morning before I forget.'

He looked amazing, she thought. His naturally tanned skin was a contrast to the white short-sleeved shirt and dark trousers and his brown eyes held hers for just a moment too long. She was deeply grateful when Paula entered and told her that she had her first four patients waiting.

'I'm not late, am I?' Cenna asked, glancing anxiously through the glass partition.

'No, they're early—and you've a couple tacked on at the end. So far.'

Phil grinned as he walked past. 'Good luck—I think we're going to need it.'

She tried to throw him a casual smile and prayed her light-hearted response sounded normal to the girls.

'Season's started early this year,' Annie said with a chuckle as she, too, hurried out. 'Thank goodness we've got Dr Prior for a bit.'

A remark that Cenna was forced to agree with as she went to her room and prepared to see her patients. Without Helen's help on Tuesdays and Thursdays they would have had to advertise for a locum. Jane certainly wouldn't be able to return when she had hoped to. Which left a question mark over the question of what they would do in the long term.

If Cenna thought the week had been chaotic to begin with, then what remained of it was organised chaos. On Friday, one entire family arrived at five-thirty as the surgery was closing. The parents and two children under ten were all complaining of sickness and diarrhoea and the woman demanded to be seen immediately.

'We're on holiday,' Shirley Marchant complained as she

sat down on the chair in Cenna's room, 'or supposed to be.'

'How can I help you?' Cenna asked, already aware of the symptoms which had been thrust at the girls on Reception.

'We've got food poisoning. I've been sick all day and so have the kids. We know exactly where we got it from. Don't we, Roger?' She glared at her husband who seemed to nod reluctantly. 'It's that hotel we're staying at—the Summerville,' she went on, brushing back her short, dark hair with an angry gesture.

For a moment Cenna paused but, allowing herself to show no recognition, asked why she thought this. The story evolved that the Marchants had last eaten a seafood salad at midday at the hotel. Since then they had apparently all suffered from nausea, vomiting and diarrhoea.

'Roger—take them to the lavatory,' the woman commanded, and obediently the husband dutifully led the children off to the loo. A few minutes later they were back and Roger Marchant informed his wife there had been no emergency.

Cenna examined each boy. She could find little wrong with either the eight- or ten-year-old, other than the older boy admitting to a 'stomachache last night' which didn't exactly fit with his mother's account. When she asked Shirley Marchant if she had kept a sample of the food that had been eaten at lunchtime, the woman glared at her.

'How were we to know it was poisoned?' she demanded.

Going on what symptoms she had found—which were very few—Cenna suggested they should eat no food for the rest of the day and drink plenty of fluids, which should include some sugar and salt to avoid dehydration.

'Is that all you're going to do?' Shirley Marchant exclaimed. 'Tell us not to eat anything and just *drink*?'

'That's the best advice I can give you,' Cenna told her.

'You haven't any sample of the food you thought was contaminated, so I can't send it for analysis. The boys haven't been sick or ill whilst here and neither have you.' Cenna wasn't convinced that either parent had the symptoms described by Shirley. Both had a healthy colour and during the half-hour that they had spent in the surgery they displayed no symptom that Shirley had complained of. In fact, she seemed in the best of health and had no trouble in voicing her opinion.

'Has anyone else at the hotel suffered a tummy upset?' Cenna asked, a question to which Shirley looked horrified.

'I haven't the least idea!' she exclaimed. 'This is ridiculous! I'm going to make a complaint to the health authorities—'

'Mrs Marchant,' Cenna interrupted calmly, 'I've examined you and your sons thoroughly and if the symptoms had led me to believe you were suffering from food poisoning—and not just a tummy upset—I would certainly take further steps—'

'I can see you just don't want to be bothered,' the woman said, standing up. 'Well, you haven't heard the last of this, I can tell you.'

Before Cenna could reply Shirley Marchant had gathered her sons and pushed them out of the room. She thought for one moment the husband was going to speak, but he, too, hurried after his wife.

'What was all that about?' Phil asked as he came in a few minutes later.

Cenna told him the whole story and he shook his head slowly.

'The Summerville?' he repeated, frowning. 'Did they get a sample of the food?'

'No.' Cenna sighed. 'She threatened to make a complaint. I wonder if she will.'

'I think perhaps we should give Mary Gardiner a buzz,' Phil said at once. 'Just in case.'

It seemed a long weekend—Phil was on call. There was no chance of them seeing one another as Phil was kept busy for most of the weekend and Ben stayed with Cenna on Sunday afternoon whilst Marcus visited Jane and the baby.

Cenna took Ben and Darren, his friend, to a movie— only because it rained mercilessly. 'Mum collects me from school now,' Ben informed her proudly as they drove to the cinema. 'She has to go back to the hospital, but Dad says it won't be for long.'

Ben's casual remark was reassuring. The boy was in high spirits when she dropped them back home in the evening and caught up on news of Jane. Marcus said the baby had gained weight and the hospital was thinking of discharging them both the following week.

The Marchants, it transpired, had packed their bags and left the Summerville on Saturday morning. They had refused to settle their bill—a fact relayed to her on Monday morning by Mary Gardiner, who was nursing a harrowing migraine.

'I need some medication,' Mary said apologetically, 'but I also felt I had to come and apologise for the trouble.'

'It wasn't your fault,' Cenna assured Mary. 'How were the two boys when they left?'

'Fine, as far as we could judge. Ray thinks Mrs Marchant was trying it on so they didn't have to pay the bill. Unfortunately we fell foul of her the first day they arrived and it was all downhill after that. She didn't like the room we gave them or the ones we changed them to. Nothing seemed to fit the bill. The food, the service, everything.'

'Well, we've had no word from the health authorities,' Cenna said hopefully. 'She didn't complain as she said she would—though, of course, we all know there was nothing she could complain of.'

'But she did write to the evening paper,' Mary said dismally. 'It's supposed to be in tonight's issue. A reporter came and we gave our side of the story. It's so frustrating, though, trying to fight your corner. She concocted a very plausible story, saying they'd had to abandon their long-awaited family holiday.'

Cenna felt truly sorry for the Gardiners. Having eaten at the place herself and seen the rooms and kitchen at first hand, she knew they were spotless. She made out a prescription for an antiemetic drug and paracetamol for the migraine and advised Mary to sleep off the worst of it in a darkened room.

The article was printed that day and unfortunately slanted towards the Marchants. 'They should have seen her sweeping in here at half five that day and demanding attention,' Annie said as she put the paper down angrily. 'I'd eat my hat if there was anything wrong with that woman.'

'It's very unfair,' Phil commented as they walked across the car park together after surgery. 'When they have worked all the hours God sent to get the business off the ground.' Then, as he paused, she almost guessed at what was coming next.

'Why don't we eat there this week?' He grinned. 'And show our support.'

'There aren't any offers on at the moment,' she told him ruefully, a gleam in her eye as she recalled the confusion of their first visit to the Summerville.

'The only offer I'm bothered about,' he replied with a straight face, 'is whether or not you'll invite me back for coffee.'

'Your suggestion of collecting Ben from school certainly helped,' Jane told Cenna as they walked from the hospital grounds towards the car park. It was a clear, bright May lunchtime and Jane, as always, was torn between making the most of her time with Ben and devoting herself to Emma. 'They feed her if necessary with my expressed milk whilst I'm away but I worry, nevertheless, that it's not from the breast.'

'I'm sure Emma doesn't really know she's missing one feed from Mum,' Cenna said as they arrived at Jane's car. 'And you can't be in two places at once.'

Jane nodded, though she felt equally disturbed when she had to leave Ben and return to the hospital. 'Thanks for helping me with these things. Hopefully, when Marcus collects us on Saturday, there won't be too much to carry. I've had to keep an entire wardrobe almost in my locker.' She unlocked the car and they both stowed the packages on the back seat.

'Is there anything else I can help with?' Cenna asked as she accompanied Jane to the driver's side.

'You've done enough already, Cenna. It was sheer heaven talking to you whilst I've been in. Five weeks seems an eternity. But Emma's a good weight now—three kilos— and she's feeding well.'

'And you're feeling rested enough to come home?' Cenna asked, her brow in a frown.

'Yes, thanks to the hospital.' Jane smiled ruefully. 'And Marcus. He's already laying down the law about me coming back to work.'

'He's right. Don't think about it until you and Emma are quite ready.'

'I know. To be honest, I still feel uncertain about leaving the hospital. I'm a doctor—a professional—but that doesn't seem to come into it when the baby is your own. The hospital staff are so reassuring. To think of going home, with the responsibility of Emma on my own shoulders...'

'Every new mother thinks that way,' Cenna reassured

her. 'And with Emma's premature birth it's only natural that you'll feel a little worried.'

Jane nodded, aware that she had promised herself a full recuperation and lots of time with the family before attempting to pick up the threads of her career. But the thought of total responsibility for Emma was still unnerving.

More than anything, Jane missed the stimulation of being with people—adults. She missed the day-to-day conversations that before Emma had made up the fabric of her life. Babies were wonderful, but it was also so important to be part of the world. It was Cenna who had kept her abreast of the more intimate pieces of news and she was deeply grateful for that.

'How's Phil?' Jane asked, unable to hide her curiosity.

Cenna looked blooming, her lovely amber eyes shining. There was an expression in them which, Jane knew, hadn't been there before.

'He's…' Cenna hesitated, then, catching Jane's curious glance, added with a shrug, 'Very well. Wonderful, in fact.'

'Ah!' Jane knew now what that expression was. 'Can I take it you two are—?'

'I haven't a clue,' Cenna interrupted carefully. 'We're just taking one day at a time.' She laughed ruefully. 'Except that we do have a legitimate date on Saturday. At the Summerville, would you believe?'

'Laying the ghosts of past Summervilles?' Jane suggested wryly, but was surprised when Cenna recounted the episode of the Marchants and the unpleasant article in the evening paper.

'So you're going for a meal,' Jane prompted slowly, 'to support Mary Gardiner and her husband. And…?'

Cenna looked at her friend from under her dark lashes. 'And that's all—for now.'

They both began to laugh until eventually Cenna glanced

at her watch and said she had to fly for surgery at two. As Jane watched her friend hurry to her car and drive away, she hoped with all her heart that the blossoming romance between Phil and Cenna would take off.

But Cenna had been hurt before. Just as she had. Eight years ago Marcus had married a mutual friend for the sake of Ben—and at the time, although in love with Marcus herself, Jane had supported his decision.

After Katrina's death circumstances had separated them and the long years that had intervened had never dulled the ache in her heart. Marcus had been her only love. But when they'd found each other again, the road had still not been easy.

Jane sighed. At least she and Marcus had Ben to cement their relationship whereas there had been no children involved in Phil's and Maggie's marriage. Her own life would have been sadly lacking without Ben's love.

Cenna would make a wonderful wife and mother. She also hoped Phil would recognise that fact. She knew he valued their working relationship. If there was a chance for Phil to forget Maggie and start again, it would be with Cenna.

As Jane drove away from the hospital, she realised she had been thinking about love and romance for once—not babies. She smiled to herself. Despite the fears she had confided to Cenna, her life must be returning to normal. And with a sudden feeling of joy she knew that she was ready to take Emma home.

But she didn't envy Cenna her fight for Phil's heart. Not with competition like Helen Prior.

Cenna was starting morning surgery—a quiet Saturday by normal standards. Patty Howard told her that there were just four booked appointments with one emergency.

'I've tacked him onto the end of surgery,' Patty said as

she stood in Cenna's room, handing her the soft records from the carousel in the office.

'That's fine,' Cenna told her. 'If we carry on at this rate, we should be finished by eleven.'

'And pigs might fly.' Patty grinned. 'I'll send your first one in. A TR with a cough.'

Cenna saw her first patient, an elderly man with, as Patty had correctly said, a cough. It had followed a chest infection, the patient told her. After examining him and unsuccessfully trying to ascertain his past medical history, Cenna prescribed an antibiotic to clear the infection.

'Perhaps it might be wise to reduce your smoking whilst you're recovering,' Cenna suggested as her patient complained that antibiotics never did the trick.

'I told you, I stopped,' coughed the pensioner. But Cenna had already seen the cigarettes poking out from his shirt pocket. It wasn't a very satisfactory situation and she decided not to prolong what was obviously an uncomfortable interview for him. He left, coughing all the way out of surgery, and when she saw him in the car park through her window, he was puffing heavily on a cigarette as he climbed into his car.

Her sympathies went out to him. It was a difficult habit to kick, especially in your seventies when it had been the habit of a lifetime. Not that he'd admitted the fact. But his nicotine-stained fingers had revealed the true story.

Her next two patients were straightforward—repeat prescription for the Pill and then one older woman for an inhaler. Stretching her arms afterwards, Cenna glanced at her watch and went along to the office.

'Has my emergency come in yet?' she asked Patty, who was seated at the desk.

'Yes, followed by another, I'm afraid,' Patty said. 'I thought it was too good to be true.'

Cenna smiled wryly. 'Oh, well, wheel him in.'

Patty nodded to the glass. 'Not that they seem in any hurry to see you.'

'Oh?' Cenna walked up to the Reception glass and glanced through. To her surprise it was Louise Ryman and Steven Oakman. They were engrossed in conversation. Remarkably, Steven sported a bandage on his arm, Louise one on her hand.

Cenna turned back to Patty and grinned wryly. 'It's nice to see our patients enjoying themselves.'

Patty raised her eyebrows. 'I'll say.'

Steven Oakman entered first and, pushing back the mop of auburn hair from his face, he told her that he had cut his arm whilst trying to mend the exhaust under his car. He hated hospitals, he confessed, but knew that it needed stitching.

Cenna took him to the treatment room, removed the makeshift bandage and saw that the long, dirty cut did indeed need stitching. She gave him an antitetanus shot, cleaned the wound and, whilst waiting for the lignocaine to take effect, asked about the result of his job interview.

'Not much luck,' he sighed. 'I'm still at the shop.'

'Are you enjoying it?' Cenna asked.

'Fish aren't really my interest,' he admitted. 'And business is a bit slow. People don't even realise the shop is on the quay. I keep telling Dad to advertise more.'

'You should create a website for him,' she said with a grin. 'Everyone's advertising that way now.'

'Except Dad. He doesn't rate technology.'

'We all have to move with the times,' Cenna remarked, pulling a face at the computer.

When all was completed, he was about to leave when Cenna reminded him to return in a week to have the stitches removed.

'OK.' He smiled. 'I'll let you know if I managed to persuade Dad onto the Net.'

'I'll send your next patient in,' Patty said as Steven left.

Louise Ryman had torn the skin of her index finger on a tin-opener. Cenna also cleaned and sutured her wound. It wasn't a serious injury but because the wound was in a sensitive place she temporarily covered the finger with a tubular bandage, pushing the gauze over the end of the finger with an applicator, twisting it gently and repeating the process.

'How are you feeling now?' Cenna asked before Louise stood up.

'I'm back at school.' She shrugged. 'OK, I suppose.'

'Did your friend come to stay with you?'

'Yes—just for a week.' Louise hesitated. 'I still feel a bit depressed. I was wondering if…'

Cenna smiled. 'You'd like some medication?'

Louise nodded and Cenna keyed in a prescription for an antidepressant. She hoped it would help, but Cenna had thought Louise's recovery from the ectopic pregnancy would have been swifter.

After Louise had gone, the telephone rang.

'I'll call for you at seven,' Phil said, his deep voice instantly recognisable. 'And bring your French dictionary. I always see something on the menu I can't understand.'

She laughed softly. 'I'm sure Mary will translate.'

'Cenna…?' The soft huskiness in his voice made the hairs stand up on the back of her neck. 'I've missed you.'

She ached to say the same but replied with some inane remark. It was too good a feeling, hearing that. It had been safer, easier, less threatening before they'd made love. When she'd thought he'd actually been relieved their date had been cancelled. Had she really thought that? Yes, she had. And perhaps at first she had been the one to push things along…

Instinct told her to wait now. Not rush. As Phil had once said himself, they had been moving too quickly. But inside, deep down, the truth was she felt she could die with love for him.

She couldn't imagine that he could ever feel that way about her.

The odd thing was, she knew exactly how he felt about Maggie.

The meal was wonderful—an indescribable concoction of seafood, salads, crisp, wafer-thin *pommes frites* and a dessert that melted in the mouth. The meringue and ice cream and an amazing strawberry sauce was Ray Gardiner's own secret creation, according to Mary.

However, the restaurant was deserted. There were just two other couples eating there.

'We've had several cancellations,' Mary and Ray told them afterwards as they sat in the lounge for coffee. 'It must have been the bad press.'

'I can't believe how quickly word circulated,' Ray said as he joined them and sat down with a sigh. He was a thin man and looked very stressed. 'We were just beginning to build up a regular trade.'

'The salad was brilliant,' Phil said as he sipped his coffee. 'They don't know what they're missing.'

'Thank you for being so supportive,' Mary told them. 'A lot of our custom has been local trade.' She sighed. 'The restaurant depends on it during winter.'

'Give it time,' Phil said with a reassuring smile. 'They'll come back.'

'I hope so,' Ray answered with a frown. 'Because we can't go on at this rate.'

It was a dismal conversation and when they left Phil remarked on it, too. Then, taking her in his arms in the car, he kissed Cenna and the world floated away. She put her arms around him and felt entirely selfish for being so wonderfully happy.

'My place or yours?' he said huskily as they took a breath.

'Either one. You choose.'

'Mine,' he decided. 'I want to spoil you again.'

'I'll make you coffee,' he told her when they arrived. 'Put some music on. Play something nice.'

She went to the hi-fi near the sofa and found the CDs. There was an eclectic mix. She wondered which ones were Maggie's favourites, told herself not to be ridiculous and grasped the first that came to hand.

Bach. A cello concerto.

'Perfect,' he told her, as he dabbled with the coffee-percolator, and she wondered if Bach had been 'perfect' with Maggie, too.

Then he turned and saw the expression on her face. Without words, he dragged her into his arms. 'Damn the coffee,' he growled, and carried her upstairs and laid her gently down. She kicked off her shoes, sinking back onto the bed. 'The buttons,' he whispered. 'Do they undo from here?'

She had worn a soft, pale green dress that lay lightly over her, a tiny snake of pearl buttons lying in the valley between her breasts. He leaned down and kissed them as she held his head between her hands. It was an exquisite feeling. They peaked for his kiss. When he massaged them gently with his lips, she felt his breath through the wispy material. She trembled and he slid up beside her.

There was no panic this time and when he began to unbutton the fragile buttons she stayed his hand. 'Could I borrow the toothbrush?' she managed.

He propped himself on one elbow and smiled. 'I like the way you taste.'

'I've eaten seafood.'

'So have I.'

'And strawberry meringue.'

'All the better to kiss you with.'

She drew her fingers lightly over his face, loving the feel of his grainy skin and chiselled jaw. His brown eyes melted her. They were so beautiful, like doe's eyes, large and dreamy, though now they were filled with desire, the thick dark lashes unable to hide the fire beneath.

Cenna wanted Phil beyond measure. She arched involuntarily and his mouth was on hers. Suddenly it didn't matter about the toothbrush. Her body had refused to wait and all the good intentions she'd had of behaving herself disappeared.

They shed their clothes quickly, she helping him to undo the buttons of her dress and he the belt she was fumbling over.

It didn't matter that the bedside light was on. Or that the little silver-framed photograph was under it.

Or that the coffee they had put on downstairs was ready.

Or that neither of them had brushed their teeth.

Love came like a tidal wave, engulfing them.

After that night, life fell into a kind of pattern. Not a very regular one, but a pattern of sorts. They grabbed the occasional lunchtime and a snack at the Fisherman's Haunt, stayed overnight at each other's houses when they weren't on call. They even managed another meal at the Summerville, hoping business had improved for Mary and Ray.

It had, marginally. But only because of the visitors. The locals they had taken a year to woo had disappeared.

Homer Pomeroy returned and was behaving himself. But he was grumpy and complained about his medication. Louise Ryman and Steve Oakman had both come back to have their stitches removed but Cenna had been out on her calls and Gaynor Botterill, the practice nurse, had attended to them.

Surgeries were busier than ever. More temporary residents signed on, and despite Helen's two days the other three and a half were fraught. Jane was home with Emma, but she was breast-feeding and Marcus said she was looking forward to July and the holidays with Ben.

May turned into a blazing June. On a Tuesday lunchtime that saw temperatures soaring, Cenna bumped into Helen as they left the surgery.

'Lunch-break or calls?' asked Helen as they walked across the car park towards their cars.

Cenna checked her wrist-watch. 'I've half an hour to clear my head then surgery at two.'

'Me, too. I thought I'd go down to the harbour. Have a cold drink at the little café there. Why don't we go together?'

Cenna hesitated. She had been trying to conquer her feelings about Helen. Had attempted to accept Helen's presence at the surgery without those pangs of jealous emotion that made her ashamed of herself for being so human, so fallible. She had tried to balance these with her reluctance to become involved with Phil. Yet, for all her endeavours, she felt that she had failed.

'Yes, why not?' she heard herself saying over-brightly.

'Come in my car if you like. The parking will be cheaper,' Helen suggested.

Cenna found herself, almost without thinking, sitting next to Helen in her jazzy racing green sports car. The roof was down and the wind blew in her dark hair. Again Cenna found herself comparing Helen and Maggie. Two beautiful women with a striking resemblance. Though she tried not to dwell on it, Cenna was relieved when Helen found a parking space outside the café.

'Waiting limited to thirty minutes,' Helen commented as she glanced at the notice, locked the car and flicked on the safety device. 'Enough time for us.'

They sat under the umbrellas outside. A full view of the

harbour spread out in front of them. 'It's gorgeous, isn't it?' Helen said as they drank from tall glasses of pure orange juice. 'Stockton hasn't any views like this to offer. I'll miss coming to Nair when Jane returns.'

Cenna was on the point of speaking when she realised that Helen had given her a quick glance. She thought the remark was probably quite innocent and decided not to comment.

This seemed not to concern Helen as she continued. 'Phil has mentioned that Jane might not be returning…'

Cenna glanced at Helen. 'Has he?'

'Yes, just a few nights ago. We were talking about Maggie. The subject cropped up of how he'd like to spend more time away from the surgery. We were looking at the albums. Perhaps it reminded him of the past. I'm not sure. Anyway, quite frankly, I've been thinking of leaving Stockton. I've been there ten years now and feel I'm due for a change. If there was an opening in Nair I'd be tempted to consider it.'

Cenna was trying to digest all that Helen had said without looking shocked. Phil hadn't mentioned this to her—but, then, why should he? Had Helen visited the house in order to see the albums? Then, perhaps most startling of all, Helen's hint that she might move to Nair.

'You knew Maggie,' Cenna said haltingly, not quite sure why she was asking the question.

'Yes. She and I got on rather well. I knew Phil before they were married.' She paused. 'It was very tragic. I don't think Phil's faced up to her death yet. I'd like to be able to help but, well…' She shrugged under the expensive-looking white fabric of her light summer suit. 'She was unique. Amazingly beautiful, don't you think?'

'I didn't know her very well,' Cenna said, her heart beating fast.

'Maggie didn't mix much, that's true,' Helen agreed. 'You started at Nair after Phil's marriage, didn't you?'

Cenna nodded slowly. 'Nair was my first real permanent job after qualifying. I moved down from the Midlands.'

'And you'll stay in Nair, of course.'

It wasn't so much a statement as a question. Cenna looked at Helen. With a sudden clarity that caused all her old doubts to return, she realised it was a question she had been asking herself for some time, albeit unconsciously.

What would happen if things didn't work out between her and Phil? Could they ever go back to the way they were? The answer was very clear now that someone else had asked it.

CHAPTER NINE

THEY didn't have time to meet all that week. Cenna tried not to let what Helen had said play on her mind. Phil didn't mention his meeting with Helen and neither did she ask. There wasn't the time—or the place. She told herself she was being unreasonable. And she knew she was. But she couldn't stop herself from dwelling on it.

In the first place, if Helen were to join the practice, all five partners would have to agree. At least in theory. Was it her own personal feelings towards Helen that were colouring her professional judgement? she wondered.

The questions went around in her mind. Had Helen really bumped into her by accident that day? Why had she suggested Cenna go with her to the harbour? Had their discussion been just a friendly chat or orchestrated?

Cenna arrived at the conclusion it had been the mention of the albums that had hurt most. Helen's visit to Phil's house. Why would Helen have gone there? Cenna had been to Phil's house numerous times now, but had never seen any albums. She hadn't any idea where he kept them.

As the days passed, Cenna finally consigned Helen's remarks to the back of her mind. It was a hectic week; the hot weather brought people off the beach in droves. Sunburn was widespread and, despite media warnings, the surgeries produced at least one casualty per session.

The heat made people irritable and short-tempered and by the end of Friday she was pleased to go home.

Not so pleased when she arrived at her house to see two men standing halfway along the path. As she pulled the car into the kerb, Phil and Mark turned to frown at her arrival.

With a sigh, she got out of the car and walked towards them. 'Phil...I didn't know you were calling...' she began, but the dark expression on his face stopped her.

'I called by on the off chance,' he replied abruptly. 'It's nothing that can't wait.'

'You're not leaving?' she asked.

'You've company,' he reminded her sharply.

'I think we have some unfinished business to resolve,' Mark said as he approached.

Cenna stared at him. 'Mark, I thought I made myself plain after our last meeting.'

'I understood that you were still angry, yes,' he replied. Glancing at Phil, he added, 'We need to talk—in private.' She realised then that she found everything about Mark unpleasant—his thin and selfish mouth and his air of self-satisfaction. For a moment she stared at him, unable to believe that he was pestering her in this way. But it wasn't until Phil spoke that she realised just how angry she was.

'Do you want me to go?' Phil asked her.

'Of course not,' she told him. Turning back to Mark, she said crossly, 'I've no idea why you came but, please, leave.'

'You don't mean that.' Mark half laughed.

'I think you heard her,' Phil muttered darkly, stepping towards him. 'It's time you left.'

Cenna saw the anger flare in Mark's eyes. For a moment she wondered if he would challenge Phil. But the moment passed and with a final glance of contempt thrown her way, he turned and strode down the garden path.

As Mark's car roared away, Cenna sighed and turned to Phil. 'Thank you,' she said quietly.

'What did he mean, that he understood you were still angry?' Phil asked her as they walked towards the house.

She unlocked the front door and they stepped in. 'We quarrelled last time we met. He told me that he was leaving for America and I—foolishly—agreed to have dinner with him—as you saw.'

'Foolishly?' Phil was staring at her and she realised that he was very angry.

'Yes, foolishly. Our relationship was over a long time ago—'

'The night I saw you at the Summerville, it didn't look that way.'

'Phil, it was a mistake, that's what I'm trying to tell you.'

'You sent the wrong person away,' he responded in a gravelly voice. 'That young man obviously believes you and he have unfinished business. He told me before you arrived that he was going to ask you to join him in America.'

Cenna stared at him, then gave a short laugh. 'Phil, that's ridiculous.'

'He didn't seem to think so.'

'Phil, I'm telling you—there's nothing between Mark and I.'

He stared at her, his dark eyes burning into hers, an expression on his face that made her tremble inside. How could she convince him she was telling the truth? But he was already turning, his fingers reaching out for the door. And in just a few seconds he was striding down the path, his broad shoulders hunched as he jumped into his car.

Pride stopped her from going after him, and when he had driven off she leaned back against the door. Why had they quarrelled so bitterly? What had possessed Mark to tell Phil that? And why had Phil chosen to believe Mark instead of her?

Should she ring Phil on his mobile? She thought about it and decided to give herself time. She turned off the answering machine, took a shower and ate some supper.

By ten o'clock that night he still hadn't rung.

*   *   *

It was the next morning before Cenna heard from Phil. He was speaking from the practice where he was taking the Saturday morning surgery. She knew at once there was something wrong by the tone of his voice. 'I'll have to make this brief,' he told her. 'My next patient is on his way in. I had a call yesterday from Gwen Derwent. Maggie's father has died.'

'Oh, Phil, I'm so sorry.' It was a few moments before she understood. She had been expecting him to refer to Mark.

'It was on Thursday night. He's not been well for some time. As you know, I was going to visit him a few months ago, but he wasn't up to it then.'

'Is Gwen coping?'

'I'm going up to stay for a few days. Maggie was an only child.'

'How sad.' She hesitated, trying not to sound selfishly disappointed. 'You were close to them, weren't you?'

'Yes—I'm travelling up this afternoon, immediately after I finish here.'

'When will you be back?'

'The funeral is on Tuesday. I rang Helen and she's coming in on Monday to cover for me.' He was brisk, matter-of-fact. The mention of Helen hurt but Cenna knew he must be aching inside and she wanted to reach out and hold him.

'Is there anything I can do?' It was all she could think of to say.

'No…nothing.'

'I'll miss you,' she said.

His tone returned to a formal note. 'I'll be in touch,' he muttered.

When she'd replaced the phone she felt empty. The incident with Mark, she felt, had driven a wedge between them. Neither of them had referred to it over the phone.

She ached to talk to him and try to explain. But she would just have to wait—and hope.

The house seemed to echo her unsettled thoughts. There was nothing she could put her mind to and she wished for once that she was on call. By Saturday evening she was already missing him dreadfully and by Sunday the moments were crawling by.

He rang her on Sunday evening, but said very little. She knew things must be tough and they didn't speak for long. At least she went to bed knowing he had telephoned.

As she lay there she asked herself how she would have felt if he hadn't rung. She could only assume she would have felt pretty desperate, a thought that didn't help one iota as she tried to fall sleep.

On Monday, Helen took Phil's surgery.

'I'm glad Phil rang me,' Helen told her as they met briefly in the staffroom. 'I was glad to be of help. Maggie's father was a dear man.' Had Helen known the Derwents? Cenna wondered. Cenna didn't want to dwell on it—she and Phil had quarrelled enough. She didn't want to think about either Helen or Maggie at this point in her life.

The rest of Monday there was no time to pause. The evening surgeries continued until six and then there were calls to make. When she arrived home, she dashed to the telephone but there were no messages on the answering machine.

There were, however, two telephone calls during the evening. One was from a friend who was still trying to persuade her into the Crete holiday. The other was from Jane who was totally captivated by the baby.

On Tuesday evening Cenna waited for the doorbell to ring. Instead it was the phone.

'I'm staying another night,' Phil told her abruptly. 'John's covering for me tomorrow.'

'I would have, if you'd asked.'

'Thanks. But you've your hands full with TRs.'

It was true, she had taken more temporary residents than anyone else. But it would have been nice to have been asked.

'How are you?' She ached to be in his arms.

'OK,' he answered tiredly.

Suddenly tears were welling up in her eyes. 'Hurry home,' she murmured, not trusting herself to say any more. Then the line went dead.

Wednesday was an eternity. The weather confounded everyone and it poured. Rain, at least, meant there were no beach casualties. Gaynor Botterill, the nurse, had a 'Stop Smoking and Stay Well' clinic. Both were new initiatives and the surgery was buzzing.

She had almost completed her list when Annie knocked. 'You don't know if Dr Jardine will be coming in, do you, Dr Lloyd?'

'No,' Cenna replied uncertainly. 'I don't. Does John?'

Annie shook her head. 'No. It's just that Mr Gardiner—'

'From the Summerville?'

'Yes. He's in Reception and specifically wanted to see Dr Jardine. He said it's important.'

'I'll see him or, if it's really important that he sees Dr Jardine, perhaps you could take a message. I know he's arriving back from Oxford today but I don't know when.'

Annie nodded, raising her eyebrows. 'I'll ask.'

A few minutes later Ray Gardiner walked into her room. He sat down with an apology then lifted his eyes to meet hers. 'I wanted to see Dr Jardine because…' He stopped, obviously finding it difficult to go on. 'Because of personal problems,' he said eventually, 'and I asked him not to make a record of it. He made an appointment for me to see a specialist but I didn't go. Mary and I had the devil of a row about it. Added to the worry of the business…' Ray shrugged his lean shoulders. 'Mary and I are under a great deal of pressure. We sat down and had a long talk at the weekend. I realise I'll lose her if I don't do something. I promised I would talk to Dr Jardine again. I came in yesterday and they said he'd be back today.'

'I see.' Cenna sighed. 'Well, due to unforeseen circumstances Dr Jardine has been delayed. He'll almost certainly be back tomorrow. '

'It took all my resolve to come here today,' Ray Gardiner said, his gaunt face looking tired and pale. 'I don't know that I can do it for a third time running.'

Cenna had no notes to refer to. Looking at her distraught patient, she frowned. 'Do you have your appointment card from the hospital?'

'No. I'm afraid I threw it away.'

'If I can make you another appointment, would you attend?'

Ray thought about that. 'I'm not sure.'

'Do you feel able to tell me—briefly—what's wrong?'

Ray heaved a sigh. 'What's wrong is that I'm unable to please Mary sexually. I have a large cyst on my testis. It's very unsightly and I'm self-conscious about it.'

'And your consultant's appointment was made with a view to surgery?'

'Yes. Dr Jardine said that the operation to remove it should be straightforward, but...' There was a long pause before he continued. 'Mary and I decided not to have children years ago. I had a vasectomy. In fact, it was the vasectomy that started off my horror of hospitals. I dread them. To be honest, I'm terrified.'

'That's very honest of you,' Cenna told him. 'Many people feel that way. But once admitted to, the fear often subsides.'

'Well, I'm doing this for Mary. I don't want to lose her.'

Cenna said she would do all she could, and after he left she telephoned the hospital. It wasn't difficult to identify the consultant and she was then able to speak to his secretary. Hopefully, she was told, a fresh appointment could be made.

As Cenna prepared to leave the practice, she hoped the Gardiners' run of misfortunes would change. They were nice people and deserved a little luck.

She was still thinking about them when she arrived home. The rain was still falling and the evening was overcast. She wondered where Phil was as she opened her front door. Had he arrived home yet? Would he ring?

Much later that evening, she was about to step in the shower when the front doorbell rang. Wrapping herself in a thick white bath towel, she padded downstairs barefoot and across the hall. Through the spyhole, she saw Phil's face and she opened the door.

'I'm wet,' he told her. Despite the short sprint from the car, he was soaked. And he looked exhausted. His tall frame looked thinner and his dark eyes had large, dark shadows beneath them. She took it all in at one glance, but when he stepped in he pulled her quickly into his arms.

'I'll change,' she whispered, as his mouth came down hungrily over hers.

'Don't go,' he muttered into her hair, brushing kisses over her neck and face.

'How's Gwen?'

'Devastated. They were married for half a century. But she'll cope.'

'Is she alone?'

'She has good friends. But it still doesn't take away the pain.'

He buried his face in her neck and she held him, not moving.

'I'm sorry,' he whispered. 'That quarrel we had...it's been on my mind...'

'Me, too,' she whispered, holding his face between her hands. 'Let's forget it.'

'Can we?'

She kissed him and nodded. 'Come and sleep.'

He bent his head and kissed her. She knew that sleep would come later. They went upstairs to the bedroom and for a few incredible hours were lost to the world.

The noise of the rain had finally stopped. Cenna gazed up at the ceiling, watching the early morning light penetrate the corners of the room. She would have to take the morning-after pill. They had taken no precautions with their love-making, their desire too intense to stop and think.

Putting her concerns to the back of her mind, she rose and looked out of the window. The trees were shimmering wetly and were very green. Quietly she went downstairs and made tea.

Phil was stirring as she came back up and lowered the mug to the bedside table. 'Hi,' she whispered as she sat down on the edge of the bed. 'Sleep well?'

He grinned, his eyes drugged with sleep. But he looked better. Less harrowed. He heaved himself up on the pillows and gulped down the tea.

'Wonderful. But not as wonderful as you,' he told her.

She leaned forward and kissed him. Dark stubble covered his jaw, an echo of the tight black curls weaving their way across his broad chest. His olive skin contrasted against the white of the bedlinen and she had to drag her eyes from the spiral of soft black hair that disappeared under the sheet.

He attempted to pull her down beside him, but she resisted. 'I didn't hear the alarm. It's almost seven.'

'It can't be.' He let her go, his hand reluctantly sliding down the sleeve of her pale green wrap. 'What's that material?'

'Silk.'

'It's very sexy.'

She grinned. 'I've showered.'

'I know. Your hair's still wet. And you smell wonderful.'

'If we want to leave for eight you've five minutes for the shower, five to dress and ten for breakfast.'

'Yes, ma'am.'

'You'll thank me later.'

He grabbed her hand as she went to walk away and pulled her down. 'We haven't talked…'

She smiled gently. 'No.'

'I missed you. God, how I missed you.'

She let out a sigh as his fingers roved inquisitively under the silk. She trembled and he held her against him and suddenly they were making love.

Her one thought was that they'd have to skip breakfast and she didn't know when he'd last eaten, but the thought lasted no longer than a few seconds, replaced by exquisite joy.

Perhaps because they were late—or because she was thinking of Phil—Cenna didn't notice the cars at the crossroad until the yellow Ford was about to turn right.

The roads were wet after the downpour during the night. The blue Vauxhall, coming in the opposite direction, skidded but couldn't stop. The crunch and tear of metal and the stomach-sinking sensation that accompanied the visual horror made her jam her foot on the brake.

She just had time to check in her mirror. Phil had stopped his car behind her. Perhaps he'd seen the two cars ahead before she had. As she swerved onto the grass bank he pulled alongside her, and before she had time to think she grabbed the mobile and was yelling into it.

Leaping from his car, case in hand, Phil caught her eye. Then he was running towards the two vehicles a hundred yards ahead, his long legs taking him swiftly across the wet tarmac. The yellow Ford had bounced, like a toy, several times. Now it was on its side a good hundred yards from the crossroads.

Cenna had a mental picture of it in the air, though she knew it could have only been for a few seconds. She'd shut out the horrific crunching and grinding of metal, mechanically forcing down the wave of sickness.

The big blue Vauxhall was on its roof. A trail of glass and metal was strewn across the road in its wake. Other cars had come to a halt. Luckily traffic was minimal. Cenna had driven the long way around, following a country road in a U-shape to avoid the queues of traffic on the outskirts of Nair. Farmland bordered one side and a small wood the other.

The two cars made the road resemble a scrapyard. The hiss of the engines went on for what seemed like an eternity. Then the deadly silence…the worst. When Cenna ran after Phil she at least had the comfort of knowing the emergency services were on their way.

'Can I help?' A woman from a car that had stopped joined her. Two men from a lorry appeared by Phil. Suddenly the road seemed full of people.

'I'm a doctor,' Cenna told her, 'and so is the man there. We might need blankets, something to use as covers.'

'I'll find something.' The woman hurried away, her face white.

Phil was at the blue Vauxhall, bending down, trying to reach the occupant trapped inside. The two men went down on their knees beside him.

She just caught his glance. 'Only one. Can you manage the Ford?' he shouted.

She nodded, then turned and ran to the yellow Escort on its side. She went down on all fours and saw a hand and her heart sank. It lay limply, stretched out from under the car. She searched for a pulse, waiting longer than she knew was reasonable. The woman arrived beside her, offering a tartan blanket. Cenna got to her knees and checked the swell in her stomach. She took the blanket.

'Thanks,' she murmured.

Cenna went to the front and what remained of the windscreen. She caught a glimpse of what was inside and knew there was no hope. Two other people had arrived and the woman, in shock, began to weep quietly. A man guided her away.

There had only been one occupant, thank God. She draped the blanket over the twisted aperture. The victim was unrecognisable, but the wrist and hand had been that of a young person. Someone's daughter...wife...child?

The ambulances arrived as she approached the Vauxhall. The police were there almost immediately, followed by fire and recovery services. The road was groaning with big vehicles, flashing lights and the sound of heavy lifting equipment.

Cenna pushed her way through the small crowd. Phil had crawled through the shattered passenger window, lying on what had been the roof. She stopped, her heart beating so fast she had to make herself swallow. A wave of fear went through her. Didn't Phil realise he had put himself in danger? There was a distinct smell of rubber and the police began shifting back the onlookers who were blocking out the light.

She told them who she was and they let her through. She bent down, lying flat on her stomach to peer in through the spaces that had once been the windows. How could he do this to her? a little voice whispered.

'He's trapped and his BP's down,' Phil shouted. He was holding the head and shoulders of a man who was barely conscious. The rest of his body was trapped in the mangled metal that had been the seat, wheel and dashboard. 'I need a line, quickly!'

Cenna fought with the urge to yell at him to get out. He was putting himself in danger, the whole wreck could collapse. With an effort she tried to compose herself, knowing that Phil was a doctor—a professional. This man's life was at stake. It hadn't occurred to Phil that he was laying his life on the line to save him.

Conquering her selfish need for him to keep safe, Cenna wriggled backwards. She shakily gave Phil's instructions to the policeman and paramedic. A few minutes later they were back with the equipment. The trapped man was at an almost impossible angle inside. Cenna lay beside Phil's legs, reaching in with the apparatus.

'We need to get him out,' Phil told her, his voice muffled. 'Quickly.'

The fire crew did all they could but it was dangerous. Each time the chassis of the car moved, Phil took the weight of the man and supported him gently in his prison of metal. Cenna fought back her fear. But she couldn't silence the little voice in her head that shouted that he didn't care enough about her to look after himself.

'No chance for the other one, Doc?' a policeman asked her, as he bent down and frowned.

Cenna shook her head. 'I'm afraid not. Do you want me to come over? If you do, someone will have to replace me here, helping with the bag and intravenous.'

'No, we'll take care of it. Here's something for you to lie on. It's wet and filthy down there.' Careful to avoid the line, he pushed a coat under her and she nodded.

'Thanks. That's better,' she said in a shaky whisper.

'Shouldn't be long before we're able to lift the whole thing up,' one of the fire crew shouted as the recovery vehicle backed slowly up.

'You'll have to take it slowly, inch by inch,' Phil shouted from inside the car. 'If he falls down towards me it'll be OK, but if he goes the other way, I could lose my grip.'

'It's dangerous in there.'

'I'll risk it.'

'Can you hold on?' another policeman asked.

'I'll have a damn good try.'

The car rocked and shook and the creaking of metal was horrendous.

'Hold it there,' Phil yelled. 'I've got him. Just.'

By the time the man was free he was unconscious which, Phil remarked, was probably a blessing. On Phil's instructions the paramedics fitted a spinal splint and strapped the man to a stretcher.

Cenna's blue skirt and white blouse were soaked in the oil and grease and Phil's clothes were unrecognisable. She didn't care. Phil was out of that mess and that was all that counted.

'What are his chances?' the police officer asked quickly as they lifted the stretcher and line into the ambulance.

'Anyone's guess,' Phil said abruptly, attending to the drip. 'I'll go with him, of course.'

Cenna nodded, aware that a second ambulance was arriving. That, she realised, was for the victim of the yellow Ford, and as Phil glanced at her she met his gaze, shaking her head.

'Are you OK?' he asked as he jumped up into the ambulance.

She couldn't tell him that she had been consumed with fear for his safety, that her own selfish needs had come before the accident victim's. Instead, she nodded and smiled weakly as the doors closed. She stood there, listening to the siren and watching the vehicle leave, the adrenaline that had been pumping around her body leaving her tired and shaky.

A little later she tried to describe what she'd seen to the police officer. It seemed very vague. All she could remember was the yellow car in the air, turning over and over, and the noise of it bouncing.

'It was wet,' she said, trying hard to recall. 'The road must have been slippery and neither car seemed aware of the other.'

'Shall I have someone run you into Nair?' the young policeman asked her when he had finished his notes. 'That was tough going, wasn't it?'

She nodded. 'I'm OK.'

'What about your partner's car?'

'Oh, yes. I'd forgotten.'

'If his keys are in it, we'll have someone drop it off at the hospital.'

'Thanks. He'd be grateful.'

She walked back to her car on legs which didn't seem her own. She could still hear the heavy lifting equipment and the sound of the police radios. Sitting in her car, she took a breath and waited for a few seconds, trying to compose herself for the drive to work.

She realised they hadn't phoned in—but there hadn't been time. She lifted the mobile and pressed the buttons with shaky fingers.

'Oh, we've been worried,' Paula said on the end of the line. 'The police rang to tell us what happened. Are you OK?'

'Yes. I'm just driving in.'

'Don't hurry. Everything's under control here. I'll have the kettle on for a good strong cup of tea when you arrive.'

Which was, Cenna realised as she reversed the car and drove back the way she had come, very much what she needed to revive her. But most of all she needed to see Phil's face, to hold him in her arms.

The thought that scared her most was if they had left for work a few seconds earlier, they could have been part of that terrible scene, too.

CHAPTER TEN

'THERE'S time for a shower,' Paula told Cenna when she arrived at the practice, glancing at her dirty clothes. 'John and Marcus saw everyone this morning. And I've rebooked those who wanted to see you specifically. The kettle's on. I'll bring a mug of tea into the cloakroom for you.'

'Thanks, Paula. You know that Dr Jardine is at the hospital?'

'Yes, he rang from there. It doesn't look good, does it? And Dr Jardine said that the other car...'

Cenna nodded slowly. 'There was nothing I could do.'

Paula sighed. 'My sympathies go to the families now. It's a dreadful shock. So quick, without any warning.'

Cenna glanced at her and nodded. She realised that Paula was thinking of her young husband lost at sea some years before. Their eyes met and Cenna saw in them the grief that Paula must still feel on occasions like this.

'If anyone knows how to help,' Paula remarked quietly, 'it will be Dr Jardine.'

Whilst showering in the cloakroom, Cenna's thoughts were with Phil. He would, no doubt, talk to the relatives of the accident victims when they arrived at the hospital. It would be a difficult task and one which he would shoulder with compassion and kindness.

The thought still appalled her that they had missed being involved by only seconds. It was a selfish thought of relief. This morning she had woken up with Phil beside her, and no clue as to what lay ahead. It made their time together seem even more precious. So how had Phil felt when Maggie had died?

A young and lovely wife…suddenly gone.

As Cenna dressed in fresh clothes, kept at the surgery for eventualities, she knew that she couldn't imagine life without him now. Yet she also knew that he had sealed part of himself away. That part was still Maggie's.

Would she ever be able to reclaim it? And if she couldn't, what would she do then?

Phil told them the surviving victim of the crash was a father of three. He'd been driving to work in Southampton. The spinal injuries were what was worrying the medical team—if he recovered. They'd worked on him for six hours in Theatre and there was more to come. Phil had spoken to his wife at the hospital and also to the dead girl's relatives. It had been a harrowing time.

The police had returned for additional details to their statements. The road, they discovered, had been damp and oily where the Vauxhall had braked. If there had been no rain and no oil, it might have all been different…

Cenna was on call at the weekend. She wanted to see Phil but was concerned the pager would shriek so she called him on the phone.

'Are you OK?' he kept asking her.

She told him she was fine.

But either on the verge of sleep or just waking up, she'd recall the yellow car in the air and hear the crumple of metal, like a scene from a movie. And then the feeling of utter uselessness. And waste. All this accompanied by the fact that she had forgotten to take the morning-after pill. Events had driven it from her mind. She tried not to worry. But what would happen if she was pregnant?

On Monday, she had a pleasant surprise. Homer Pomeroy was her first patient. He was smiling as he came in and he looked very dapper. His grey hair was carefully swept back over his head and he wore a flawless grey suit.

For a second or two, the smell of cologne pervaded the room as he sat down.

'I'd like you to look at my leg,' he told her, 'and pronounce me fit. I need a bill of good health—at least, for the next four weeks.'

Cenna smiled wryly. 'Only four weeks?'

'Well, I'm a realist, my dear. I have a special reason for wanting to be fit. I'm taking a friend on holiday. A lady friend.'

Her curiosity must have shown because Homer chuckled. 'No, nothing as exciting as a holiday romance,' Homer admitted with a regretful sigh. 'I'm far too old to make a fool of myself again. I'm going for a month to Florida—with Mrs Vine. Thought she could do with a break after all the hard work of looking after me.'

Cenna was surprised, but relieved. 'Are you feeling well?' she asked.

At her cautious tone, Homer laughed outright. 'Yes, thanks to you, my dear, very well. I'm taking those blessed pills like sweets and haven't looked a turkey in the eye since I saw you last.'

Cenna laughed, too. 'Then I should find nothing amiss with your blood pressure today.'

Homer coughed. 'Absolutely not. Providing the machine's on its toes.'

Cenna took her patient into the treatment room where Homer removed his suit and climbed up onto the couch. Cenna found herself smiling as she wrapped the rubber cuff around her patient's arm.

'Reasonable.' She nodded. 'Better than last time.'

Homer smiled. 'I should hope so. Lot of damned hard work, all this.'

'Which I hope will continue,' Cenna remarked as she examined his leg.

'Absolutely,' Homer assured her. 'I'm keeping the celebrating to a minimum.'

'Well, your leg has improved, that's evident. I still don't like the look of the big toe, although your knee is less swollen. Try to maintain your diet whilst you're away. And I don't have to remind you of the dangers of alcohol. Having an attack whilst you were away would not only prove painful but embarrassing.'

'You do wonders for the ego, my dear.' Homer lifted himself from the couch, grinning as he caught her reproving eye. 'Don't worry, I'm going to be good. I think Mrs V. deserves a splendid holiday for looking after me the way she has. I wouldn't want to spoil it for her.'

Cenna, however, wasn't convinced. Sun, sea and hotels providing every conceivable luxury would be irresistible, surely? The only plus was that Mrs Vine would be there to keep an eye on him—a duty Cenna didn't envy her.

'Wish me luck,' Homer said rather thinly as she printed out his prescription.

'I hope you won't need it,' Cenna answered sincerely.

On Friday news came through about the driver of the blue Vauxhall. Phil came to Cenna's room mid-morning. 'He's had a rough passage, but he's stabilised. The downside is that further surgery is needed to remove pressure from the spinal cord.' He sat down with a sigh. 'In other words, it's an unstable injury and they are concerned that vertebrae may shift and cause damage.'

'Or sever the cord entirely,' Cenna said quietly.

'They haven't ruled out accumulated fluid or a blood clot.'

'So, the worst way it's paralysis?'

'The worst way is not surviving the next op.'

She paused, leaning back in her chair. 'And the positive

outcome,' she said quickly, 'would be to stabilise the affected bones. Skeletal traction perhaps?'

Phil nodded once more. 'Thank God, he had no other internal injuries.'

'And you got him out pretty rapidly.'

Phil shrugged. 'It was just luck we were on the scene.'

Cenna had thought about that, but more subjectively. She hadn't been able to dismiss the notion they might have been part of the crash. Or that working the way he had under the car had been extremely dangerous. Since then she had thought a lot about their relationship. Phil was more precious to her than she had ever believed possible. It was frightening to love so much. To know someone was your whole world. And that losing them was unthinkable.

'Hey—where are you?' Phil was speaking, amusement in his eyes.

'Sorry. What did you say?'

'I just made you an offer I thought you wouldn't be able to refuse.' He laughed, leaning forward. 'But I was wrong. You ignored me entirely.'

'Make the offer again.' She smiled. 'And whatever it is, I'll say yes.'

'Fair enough.' His dark eyes held hers. 'I checked with the rota. In seven days' time we have the weekend off.'

'Both of us?'

'Together,' he confirmed.

She smiled. 'That sounds heavenly.'

'Let's get away. Right away. Let's get lost.'

She laughed. 'Where?'

He shrugged. 'The country. A quiet little village somewhere. A four-poster with a ghost.'

'I'll settle for the four-poster,' she told him. 'I'm not so certain about the ghost.'

He rose and came round the desk. Pulling her up into

his arms, he bent his head and kissed her. Softly, then with a sudden passion.

'I'm misbehaving,' he growled.

She nodded. 'We both are.'

He let her go reluctantly. 'We'll go on the Friday evening, come back Sunday night.'

She grinned. 'Remember, no ghosts.'

'Scout's honour,' he told her as he walked to the door.

'Phil?'

He turned and she swallowed. 'Nothing, just…' She wanted to tell him that she loved him, but knew that would spoil everything. 'It will be lovely,' she said instead.

His smile told her she had said the right words. When he'd gone, she sat quietly, deep in thought. His expression had revealed nothing that could tell her what he was thinking. But his smile had seemed to hold relief.

Doubts filled her. She couldn't imagine a future without him. But what if she had to? What if she was pregnant? What if all he could give her was part of him? Could she accept that? An affair—a protracted affair—as, in all honesty, it would be. And a child to think about…a new life created…or spurned.

She would face those questions…soon. But not yet. Not until she found the strength.

'Furzey Bassett…' Cenna pointed to the road sign. 'Down there, that little lane. You'll never get through.'

'Just you watch me.'

'There's a tractor.'

'Damn.'

'You're giving in again.' She was trying to stop laughing. It had been the pattern of the day as Phil slung one long arm across the back of her seat and twisted to frown out of the rear window. The whine of the engine subsided to a growl as he slung the car into an opening. The tractor trundled by, the driver grinning.

It had been wonderful so far. They had got lost and found themselves a dozen times. Discovered miniature, leafy lanes that wound into farms and woods. Reversed out of roads into boggy ditches and become cattle-bound, with doleful brown and white heads bobbing past the car.

'Another world,' Phil had remarked. It couldn't have been truer. Little villages clustered together, linked by busy roads that seemed to have no connection to the rural idyll. Just arteries that drove the lifeblood into the heart of the countryside.

'Where are we going now?'

Phil grinned as they watched the tractor disappear. 'Follow him?'

'Definitely not.'

'What about there?'

She looked across the lane. A small path, barely enough to squeeze the car along, beckoned them. 'It's private, isn't it?'

'There's no gate. Nothing to say we're trespassing.' He put the car into first gear and edged out slowly. Fringes of grass and wild flowers obscured the way. The smells of cattle and pig manure washed in the open window.

'What if it's a dead end and there are only fields?'

'Then I'll carry you into the field and make love to you there.'

'You'll have to catch me first.'

'Now you're talking.' They were both laughing, being fools and loving it. The practice seemed light years away and, for Cenna, so did Maggie. She hated to admit it, but ever since Friday evening when they'd set off, her shadow had receded. It might be imagination, she told herself.

But she knew it wasn't. Phil had driven them deep into the countryside, first through Hampshire, then into

Wiltshire. They had talked and laughed and driven on, without the map.

Finally, it had been the sunset that had stopped them. A panorama of burning colour. They'd parked on the top of a hill. Below them had been the lushest of valleys. They'd got out and sat, arms linked, on the grass. To the song of the birds, the great scarlet orb had descended, a furnace of gold.

It had only been hours they had been away. It had felt like light years. As if they'd always been part of the hill.

'We're communing with nature,' Phil murmured as peace and tranquillity filled them.

'It's healing,' she whispered.

'And humbling. To be alive and part of all this...'

They watched the last rays of purple and gold turn to a milky dusk. They left then, though they didn't want to.

Risking it, they stopped at the first country hotel they came across and miraculously found a room.

The bed wasn't a four-poster, but it was cosy, timber-beamed and sumptuous smells came from the small restaurant.

'No ghost,' Phil told the receptionist.

'None that we know of,' they were assured.

Their supper was delicious, as was the drink at the bar afterwards.

'Is there anything else you'd like to do?' Phil asked her as they walked to the staircase. 'Walk, talk? Go on somewhere else?'

'You know what I want,' she said softly, wrapping her arms around his waist.

'I know what I want,' he muttered. 'But, then, I'm a selfish brute and I've only got you to myself for two days.'

'And two nights.'

'Maybe three if you stay with me on Sunday.'

For a moment she wasn't sure about that. She didn't want

to think of reality, waking from the dream. And she didn't want to think of Phil's house, which always stamped part of him as Maggie's and the past.

The noise of someone coming along the hall made him draw away. They giggled, like teenagers. Then without a word, they climbed the staircase. Their love-making was wonderful, passionate and free and without the clock ticking inevitably away.

The morning had burst in through the window, inviting them to explore. The breakfast was incredible. Too large for Cenna to finish. Phil ate her bacon and a sausage under the pretext of needing an energy top-up. After that, the lanes and fields and little tracks were their own.

Cenna's thoughts were brought back to reality as the lane came to an abrupt end.

'You're right. It's a dead end.'

'A beautiful dead end.'

The tall swaying trees were amazing, cresting the hill; great oaks and sycamores, an umbrella of green that flowed over their heads.

She said with a sigh, 'I wish we had a picnic.'

'I have you,' he told her, and when she looked at him he wasn't smiling. He took her in his arms and kissed her, his hands lifting her chin. 'And I've a blanket in the boot.'

'And there's a field…'

He nodded slowly. 'Who could ask for more?'

They made love under the trees, careless of the farmer who never arrived and the cattle who apparently weren't grazing. There was only the soft July breeze and the caw of the rooks above. It was so beautiful, neither of them spoke. Their desire made up for words, their bodies entwined, a part of nature.

On Sunday morning they ate a leisurely breakfast, then packed and reluctantly left the hotel.

It was hot and there wasn't a cloud in the sky. They had the windows down in the car and at the first big road sign Phil slowed the car. 'Turn left for Wales,' he said with a grin, 'or right for—'

'Home.'

'Or straight up. To Scotland.'

Cenna laughed. 'I wish!'

He turned and glanced at her. His dark eyes were serious and she shivered at their expression. 'I don't want to go back either.'

She nodded, attempting humour. But her voice was regretful as she said, 'I don't think there's time to get to Scotland and back before nightfall.'

'No, perhaps not.' He smiled. 'So where?'

'There's a mill, first left, then second right.' She pointed to a small road sign under the larger one.

'Done.' He followed the directions and they came to a double gate. A large black and white notice announced Farrington Mill, a seventeenth-century water mill and lake.

The scene was magical. Four acres of forest and a preserved and running water mill, hidden under a large arch of cream stone, topped by a waterfall of vine and creepers. Next to the mill was a half-timbered café, a shop and a little museum, and beyond this a lake. The curling ribbon of water glistened and beckoned enticingly.

'It's beautiful,' she sighed as they walked towards it. They spent an hour trekking around it, unable to forage in the wilder part because they had worn shorts and sandals. But down by the shore the water lapped smoothly into the grassy banks. They sat and watched the fish, silvery trout that spun circles in the water.

They leaned against a willow that spilled its green fronds into the water and he pulled her gently against him. 'We're the only ones here.'

'It's early yet.'

'We'll walk around the other side and eat at the café afterwards.'

'I warn you, I'm ravenous.'

He laughed aloud. 'You can't be. We've just had breakfast.'

She laid her head in his lap. 'That was two hours ago.'

He trailed a sliver of grass around her face, his fingers tracing the outline of her features. Suddenly that odd expression came into his eyes. 'I can't believe how easy it is for you to eat.'

She laughed. 'That's what you do when you're hungry—you eat.' Then she stopped, realising. 'Oh, Phil, I'm sorry—how thoughtless of me. I'd forgotten—Maggie's condition…'

'I suppose it still gets to me…' His voice was soft, his eyes meeting hers. 'One is always so conscious of that word—eating—when you live with someone who's anorexic. It never really comes into your vocabulary—except with a certain amount of trepidation. Maggie hated eating out and so we never did. And at home we rarely ate together. I gave up, you see. It caused problems if I insisted she eat.'

'It was as bad as that?'

He nodded. 'Yes, eventually.'

'Did it happen because of her modelling?'

'I don't think so. Gwen said they'd had a lot of trouble when she was younger.'

'Wasn't she getting better, didn't you say? When you married?'

His face grew tense. 'I didn't know it was anorexia. I should have, of course. But she was very good at…camouflaging. So I don't really know whether she had improved—or whether I wanted to think so. With my odd hours, too, she would often say she'd eaten, so I assumed she had. It was only when she seemed to be getting thinner that my suspicions grew.'

'She was working, then?'

He nodded. 'Modelling for a catalogue. In London. Sometimes we'd go for days without actually sitting down together, let alone eating a meal at the same table.'

Cenna sighed as she looked into his grave, hollowed face. It held so much in its features—the pain and the loss and the depth of love that he must have had for her. And being unable to help—she understood that only too well from the car accident. She hadn't been able to help that poor girl and it had been such a waste. How much more did Phil feel for his dead wife?

'Her parents must have been devastated.'

'Yes, they were, but…' He paused, removing a dark strand of hair from her cheek and tucking it behind her ear. 'I think they accepted her condition more than I was able to. Which is ridiculous, because I'm a doctor. I'd seen it before, I knew there was treatment and it could be successful. Gwen said, when I saw her last, that they suspected her reason for marrying a doctor was an unconscious cry for help.' He leaned his head back against the tree. 'But I just didn't hear.'

She sat up, taking his hand. 'Phil, you did everything you could. You can't blame yourself.'

His dark eyes were shuttered as he lifted his head. 'Oh, but I do. Who else was there for her to turn to?'

'Her therapist, consultant, counsellor…?' Cenna said, recalling Phil had told her that Maggie had finally sought treatment.

'But I was closest.'

'Sometimes being close makes you blind.'

He gave her a little grimace. 'I could have done more.'

'Like what? Maggie was hiding the truth.'

He squeezed her hand and, drawing her into his arms,

dropped a kiss on her forehead. 'Anyway, that's all in the past,' he said quietly. 'And today is ours. Let's walk.'

Cenna wanted to just lie there and listen. She wanted him to talk about Maggie, exorcise her. She wanted to be able to deal with a reality and not a ghost. But he pulled her to her feet and kissed her, effectively silencing her.

As they walked, once again Maggie was with them. As long as he kept her in his heart, achingly preserved in regret, she would always be there. As they strolled round the lake, she had never felt Maggie's presence so deeply. No matter how hard she fought to keep him, it felt as though Maggie always drew him back.

It was half past nine when they reached Nair. Around the coast there were little twinkling stars of light, dazzling if looked at for too long. A crescent moon shone clearly over the dark water and a July breeze held nothing in it but a gentle whisper.

'Are you coming home with me?' Phil asked as he drove.

'I'm tempted…'

'But you won't.'

Cenna glanced at him and smiled. 'Only because we're shattered. And I've my clothes to sort out—'

'And so it's no?' His tone was gentle and she knew he was tired, too. They hadn't talked about Maggie again, despite brave attempts on her part.

'Come in and have coffee.'

'Once upon a time I would have thought that a very special invitation.' He grinned. In the dusk she could barely see his features. But she knew he was smiling.

'It still is.'

'So what if I refuse to leave after coffee?'

'I'd accept your refusal.'

'You're not making this easy.' He took the road to her house. In the moonlight, the houses looked inviting, lights flicking on. When they drew up beside the gate, he sighed. 'The last time I was here, I had an interesting conversation with someone who was very intent on seeing you.'

'Oh,' she said dully, knowing instantly who he meant. 'Mark.'

'I hate to say this, but I was right, wasn't I?'

She looked at him and gave in. 'He thought—'

'That you were more than just *old friends*?' he interrupted as he pulled on the brake and turned off the engine.

She nodded. 'I just didn't see it. I realised it when you told me he was going to ask me to go to America.'

'And I stormed off, like an idiot,' Phil murmured on a sigh.

She reached across and slid her hand between his fingers. 'Let's go in for that coffee.'

'Tempting.'

'But you won't.'

'Let's just say that if I do, I shan't be leaving again before tomorrow morning.'

Something she felt had shifted, a subtle difference in their relationship that she couldn't quite identify, and she didn't argue the point when he next spoke.

'I'll walk you to the door.' He leaned towards her and she slid her arms around his neck. He smelt intoxicating; his own personal aroma and the cologne that she would have been able to identify blindfolded. 'It's been wonderful,' he whispered, kissing her mouth. His lips were warm and inviting.

'Very wonderful.' She kissed him back, pulling his head down, and a small groan escaped from his lips.

'You'd better not do any more of that…'

She leaned her forehead against his. 'I'll miss you.'

He smiled. 'I hope so. Come on, before I ravish you here.'

When Phil had walked her in, she listened to the car until

the sound disappeared into the night. She went in and turned on the lights and opened the French doors. It was a heavenly evening. She walked slowly onto the grass and sat on one of the steamer chairs. The scents were intoxicating. She was reminded of the lovely old mill and the lake. Cenna had understood then, about Maggie.

If he had wanted to break her spell he would be here now, insisting he stay the night, making love to her with all the intensity that she had for him. With a sharp pang of awareness, Cenna accepted that she had come to the point where the truth couldn't be ignored.

She would have to settle for far less than the depth of her own love if she wanted to keep Phil. And she wasn't certain, this evening, if she could settle for less. Not unless she was pregnant. And even then…she sighed deeply. She just didn't know…

CHAPTER ELEVEN

OVER the next few weeks Cenna grew accustomed to Phil's tap on the door. He would take her in his arms without a word and lead her up to the bedroom.

His love-making was intense, too desperate at times. Too unbelievably satisfying. She knew she shouldn't worry. It was ridiculous to be concerned over something so good. But because it was just that, she did. It was hard to live for the moment. Fears of the future always seemed to creep in.

The only real time she felt he was himself was when he was making love to her. She always hoped she'd find the real Phil there afterwards. The man who brought her such incredible physical pleasure and joy. That when they left that world, she could keep possession of him. But he seemed to retreat.

Not consciously—but retreat he did. Away from her.

Surgery was hectic. Temperatures soared and temporary residents signed on every day. By the end of July, Cenna found that she was seeing an increasing number almost certain to escalate further.

Phil called a staff meeting at the beginning of August. The weather had turned and a fresh wind and spots of rain started to fall as, at seven-thirty on a Friday evening, all members of staff took their seats in the staffroom.

'We've one or two things in particular on the agenda,' Phil said, standing up and thrusting a hand through his hair. 'First and foremost, the temporary residents. This year we're handling more numbers than ever.' He nodded to Helen in the front row, and Cenna sitting several rows back watched as Helen smiled up at him. 'Helen has kindly

148

agreed to stay on until the end of September to help us out, but we're still going to be hard-pressed. My suggestion is, that we—the doctors, that is—start a half an hour earlier in the mornings, or go on thirty minutes later for August.'

'As normal, then,' Marcus chuckled at the end of the row.

Phil grinned. 'Yes, I have to admit that lately we've been running over time.' He looked at Cenna. 'How do you feel about that, Cenna? And you, John?' He glanced at John who was seated next to Cenna.

'Either way, it's fine by me,' John agreed.

'Me, too.' Cenna nodded.

'Marcus?'

'No problem.'

'OK, good.' Phil turned to Jean Thomas, the practice manager, who sat behind him. 'Now for holidays. Jean— over to you.'

A ripple of conversation went through the room and Cenna saw Annie and Paula lean forward in their seats to talk to Gaynor.

Jean stood up and glanced around. 'I have the list here,' she said, and began to read off the booked holidays for the rest of the year, those first of the nursing staff and reception team, all of whom looked relieved to have their chosen dates confirmed.

Cenna knew that Marcus was taking a fortnight at Christmas to be with the family and that John Hill had another week in early December.

'Cenna, you've still two weeks to take,' Jean said with a frown. 'I have you pencilled in for the last week in September and the first in October for your Crete holiday. Are you happy with that?'

Cenna glanced at Phil whose head seemed to be buried in the papers on his lap. She had brought up the subject of holidays with him and hadn't got very far. She had commented on the Crete holiday several times, hoping he might respond. There had been several cancellations from the gym club, bookings that he could have taken. But he had shown no interest. Now the trip to Crete which she had tentatively agreed to in March seemed frighteningly close. Phil hadn't suggested another break together after Wiltshire, so she had paid her deposit and sunk all her boats.

Cenna looked back at Jean and nodded.

'Good.' Jean smiled. 'Then that just leaves you, Phil.'

'I haven't given it much thought, Jean,' Phil said quietly as he lifted his head. 'I've nothing specific planned.'

Cenna's heart sank.

'OK,' Jean said quickly, glancing down at her list. 'Late November I've two weeks coming up. How will that suit you?'

'Done,' Cenna heard Phil say and she felt a tightness under her ribs.

'Now, on to other matters,' the practice manager said breezily to a loud whisper of groans. Jean smiled and glanced at her watch. 'Another ten minutes, everyone, and we should be finished. Tea and biscuits afterwards.'

Cenna sat quietly, aware that John was talking to her. She listened to him, vaguely taking in the comments he was making, her mind distracted by the fact she had now made a final commitment to her holiday and Phil to his.

As John's voice drifted over her, she realised that all the warning signs had been there for some time in her relationship with Phil. She avoided, if she could, going to his house. It was too full of Maggie, despite there being no obvious reminders—or maybe because of that. And Phil rarely suggested it now, staying at her place whenever the opportunity arose. Her little house was always welcoming, he told her. She didn't question his motives. When she'd told him she was considering the holiday abroad, he had smiled and nodded slowly. 'You'll need the break,' he had remarked gently.

'So, how do you feel about Helen joining us?' John was saying quietly.

Cenna looked into his pleasant face and frowned. 'I'm sorry?'

'Helen, as a partner,' John repeated. 'She mentioned that she's leaving Stockton. Or am I talking out of turn?'

Cenna swallowed and her gaze went to Helen. She was sitting beside Phil deep in conversation with him. 'No, you're not, John. I heard something like that, too.'

'I thought it might be on the agenda tonight.'

Cenna nodded slowly. 'Perhaps at the next meeting.'

There was a pause and he said, 'So, you're off to Crete, then?'

Cenna talked a few minutes longer but her mind wasn't really on the subject of holidays. Finally she made her excuses and left. As she went she saw Phil and Helen talking. Phil had one arm slung over the back of a chair, his broad shoulders relaxed, whilst Helen as always was talking animatedly.

When Cenna reached the cloakroom she was relieved to find it empty. She wanted to be alone and inevitably it was to Maggie her thoughts went as she sat on the small stool and faced the mirror.

Her eyes revealed the simple truth. It was terrible to be jealous of a dead woman. And yet she couldn't deny it. She was even jealous of Helen for looking like Maggie.

Then as a small tear escaped and she hurriedly swept it away, the jealousy faded. In its place was a slow, final acceptance. She had fought so hard and loved him for so long. But she was powerless to fight any longer.

It was a week later when Cenna took the second test and confirmed she wasn't pregnant. The relief was enormous, yet it was mixed with regret. Sadness for what might have been, for the life they might have created. Yet she would have felt as though she'd trapped Phil and she wouldn't have wanted that.

Her mind was still on Phil and the baby when Paula put her head around the door. 'Cenna, I'm uncertain what to do. It's Mrs Derwent—Dr Jardine's mother-in-law. I don't think Dr Jardine is aware she's visiting…he's out on his calls.'

Cenna rose to her feet and followed Paula along to the waiting room. It was relatively quiet, the last two patients of the morning still waiting to be seen. Gwen Derwent sat by the window, reading a magazine.

'Shall I leave her with you?' Paula asked uncertainly. 'I did tell her Dr Jardine won't be back until two.'

'Yes, OK, Paula.' Cenna hoped she had successfully hidden her surprise and to some extent shock because even from where she stood, Gwen Derwent looked like Maggie. She was very much like the photograph Cenna had seen in Phil's bedroom—Maggie's slim body, dark hair and, even with her head bent, a very attractive woman.

Cenna walked over and it wasn't until Gwen Derwent lifted her head that Cenna saw how mistaken she'd been. For Gwen Derwent's face was ravaged by grief and sadness. Her still attractive face was cleverly made up and helped to disguise the scars, but there was no doubt that the death of her daughter and then her husband had taken its toll. The deep lines etched around her dark, tired eyes and mouth spoke volumes.

'I'm Cenna Lloyd,' Cenna said, and stretched out her hand.

Gwen took it immediately. 'Cenna? Oh, I'm so pleased to meet you. Phillip has told me lots about you.'

'Has he?' Cenna faltered. An unreasonable flare of hope ignited inside her.

Gwen nodded. 'Yes. And all good.'

'That's a relief,' Cenna said lightly. 'Paula told you Phil's on his calls?'

She nodded. 'Yes, this is just an impromptu visit. I'm ashamed to say it's my first real excursion out of Oxford since Derek went. I lost my confidence for a bit. But I wanted to call in and let Phil know how well I was doing.' She laughed self-consciously. 'Except I have to make the drive back yet.' She smiled gently. 'Phil has been a wonderful help—as you must know. I was feeling very down. But now I'm beginning to get back on my feet.'

'I was very sorry to hear about your husband,' Cenna said softly. 'I know how close Phil is—was—to you both.'

'That's very much appreciated.' The pale blue eyes held Cenna's.

'Have you had lunch yet?'

'No...'

'If you'd like coffee, then I could drink one, too. And Paula could arrange some sandwiches. We could sit in the staffroom.'

'Are you sure? You must be busy.'

'My surgery begins at three, so the break will be welcome.'

'I'd love coffee,' Gwen agreed as she rose, 'but don't worry about the sandwiches. I can stop at the motorway services on my journey home.'

Cenna led the way upstairs.

'It's very modern and elegant here,' Gwen remarked as they walked together up the stairs.

'You must be more familiar with the old practice,' Cenna guessed.

'Yes, Derek and I visited Phillip there once. Up on the clifftop—the old crofter's cottage.'

'Far too small eventually, I'm afraid.' Cenna led the way into the staffroom.

Gwen sat down and, after making the coffee, Cenna sat beside her.

'How spacious this lovely room is,' Gwen commented. 'I'm so proud of Phillip. He wanted a new premises for so long and had such wonderful ideas before Maggie died.' She hesitated, turning the coffee-cup slowly on the saucer. 'Phil took it very badly, you know. And I'm afraid Derek and I were very little use to him at the time. Maggie was our only child.'

'Yes, Phil told me. I can't imagine what it must be like to lose a daughter.'

'Derek never really recovered. Maggie was the light of his life.'

They were silent for a moment before Gwen said quickly, 'You know, I was so worried about Phillip. But I don't feel that way any more. Not since he told me about you. He needed strength and you've given it to him.'

Again the little flame of hope flared. 'I'm glad I could help.'

'The anorexia devastated them both,' Gwen told her quietly. 'Maggie had it from a teenager, though we didn't realise. She was plump as a child. We thought she had just shed her puppy fat. It wasn't until she was sixteen that we realised something was wrong. She was painfully thin. Anorexics are very clever—as you must know. They will do their utmost to hide the problem. Maggie was very successful at deception. Poor Phillip. He had no idea before they married.'

'I don't think it would have made any difference,' Cenna replied kindly. 'He loved her deeply.'

Gwen looked at her. 'Yes, he did. He balanced her. Where Maggie was impulsive, Phillip was the steadying influence. She loved excitement. Modelling gave her that. And the opportunity to travel. She met Phillip abroad. Three months later she was married. Our hearts ached for

Phillip. He was a doctor, yes, but it's very different when the anorexic is your wife.'

Just then the door behind them opened and Phil appeared. 'Gwen! How wonderful to see you.' He hurried over and Gwen stood up, hugging him to her.

'Cenna has been keeping me company, Phillip. I'm afraid I've taken up all of her time.'

'Not at all. But I must go now.' Cenna smiled as she reached out to shake Gwen's slim hand. 'It's been lovely to meet you, Gwen.'

'Didn't I tell you I had a perfect partner?' Phil said to Gwen.

Cenna met his dark gaze, desperate to read an intimacy in his eyes, but there was none.

'You did indeed. And now I know what you mean,' said Gwen softly.

Choking back the hurt, Cenna made her exit. She was close to tears when she arrived back in her room. Phil's remark had said it all. A perfect partner. That was what she was to him and would always remain. He was content with their relationship as it was and had no desire—or intention—to further it. How could she ever have imagined that being pregnant would unite them?

'You're very quiet.' Phil took her hand as they walked along the quay. The sky was aflame with burning colour and the sea beneath a sparkling, dancing aquamarine.

'It's been a busy week,' Cenna replied lamely. She looked up at him, cherishing the time they had left together. After Gwen's visit yesterday the way was clear. First her holiday, then she would give in her notice. Phil wouldn't want to take it, of course. Their partnership, as he had told Maggie's mother, was perfect. But she would stand firm, as she knew she must.

For sanity's sake.

She knew what she wanted from the only man she had ever truly loved. His heart. She had never possessed Phil's and never would. She couldn't and wouldn't settle for less—as she had done with Mark. No. Whilst she had the strength, the same strength that Gwen Derwent had commented on, she must do the only thing left to do.

'I would ask what you were thinking, but somehow I hesitate,' he murmured softly, turning her slowly to face him. His hands cupped her bare shoulders, the dress she was wearing, a summery shift of dark blue, almost the colour of the sea.

'I was thinking of Gwen.' She answered honestly, sliding her arms around his neck, aching for him. 'She's had so much grief, yet she's such a strong woman.'

His chiselled features seemed suddenly to soften. 'Yes, I admire her tremendously. Maggie couldn't have had better parents. They were devoted to her.'

'Yes, I gathered that.'

'The trouble was—' He stopped abruptly and pulled her against him. Cupping her face between the palms of his hands, he whispered, 'The trouble is, you always make me stray from the topic I'm most interested in. And that, my darling, is you.'

She lifted her amber eyes and smiled. 'I want to know all about you, Phil. I want to understand—'

'There's nothing more to tell,' he scolded her gently, effectively silencing her enquiries once more. 'What you see is, I'm afraid, what you get.'

She knew that now. She knew she had no hope of claiming his heart. But for a brief moment she had wanted to try for one last time. He kissed her tenderly, driving away the pain briefly. 'I want you,' he whispered, 'so much.'

They walked hand in hand along the quay. It was dark now, with only the water lapping at the harbour's edge and the twinkle of lights reflected in the water. He drove back to her house, their destination without question.

She didn't turn on the lights. They didn't even make an attempt at coffee or supper. Silently they went upstairs and he held her tightly. 'I'm ashamed to admit how much I long for this during the day,' he told her, his voice rough with desire. 'I have to force myself to stop thinking about you.'

His hands reached out to help her remove her dress, then trailed over the soft swell of her breasts. 'You're so beautiful, do you know that? So womanly.'

She wondered what he had said to Maggie. What he had said when he'd made love to her. Had their passion been driven, too, by some shattering, mystical force? Had he made love to Maggie as he made love to her? Quickly she shut the thought out. They had so little time together left, she mustn't spoil it with her jealousy.

She undid his belt and shirt buttons and soon they lay beside one another, their breathing the only sound of the soft summer's night.

'What am I going to do when you're away?' he muttered, rolling over her, playing with the lacy straps of her bra.

It hurt her to hear him talk of the holiday. The question tormented her. He could have gone with her if he'd really wanted. There had been opportunity enough.

'I'll bring you back some sun.' It took all her will-power to make light of it. She had to. There was no other way.

'You're my sun,' he told her, and she was desperate to believe him. But in her heart she knew better.

Time didn't matter then—or words. His love-making utterly fulfilled her. Love-making that took her to the height of bliss, expended all her energy, and, as she lay beside him afterwards, an exhaustion that left no room for regret. Curled up, with her back against his strong chest, sleep overcame them both.

It was always the morning that brought the gentle regret. Not the regret of the past but of the future. The days, weeks and years ahead, empty without him.

It was then she had to be strong. Remind herself of what she truly wanted. No compromise with Maggie. No half-measures. It was all or nothing. And he would never give her all.

One Saturday in the middle of August, Mary Gardiner rang the surgery. It had been a busy Saturday morning, but the waiting room had finally emptied and Paula had locked up.

'Mary Gardiner on line one, Dr Lloyd,' Paula called as she was about to leave. 'She wanted to speak to Dr Jardine.'

Cenna took it immediately. Mary explained that her husband didn't feel well, but refused to come in to the surgery. Cenna said that she would call and a few minutes later she was parking in front of the Summerville.

The hotel seemed busy enough as Cenna entered the foyer, and she hoped the Gardiners' problems had been resolved. But when Mary met her and showed her into the living quarters, she was shocked to find Ray slumped in a chair, looking very sick.

'You shouldn't have called the doctor,' he said breathlessly, glancing at his wife.

'On the contrary,' Cenna told him, pulling up a chair. 'You're obviously not well.'

'It's indigestion,' he muttered. 'That new recipe with the peppers. They always react on me. The pain will go away soon.'

Cenna began her examination as Mary watched anxiously. Ray was breathless and clammy and the central chest pressure and arm pain he exhibited alerted her to more serious problems. When she discovered an abnormal heart rhythm, she wasted no time in phoning for an ambulance.

It arrived quickly and with the Gardiners both on board, Cenna followed in her car to the cottage hospital. Ray was admitted immediately to the coronary care unit. Cenna sat with Mary in the small waiting room provided for relatives.

'It's a heart attack, isn't it?' Mary said, as Cenna brought her a coffee from the machine.

'Ray had ventricular fibrillation,' Cenna explained. 'It means an abnormal rhythm which interferes with the heart's pumping action.'

'Will they be able to stop the irregular beat?' Mary asked.

'They'll control it with drugs or electrical defibrillation,' Cenna explained. 'And he'll have other tests, even an angiography if necessary.'

'He's been under the weather lately,' Mary said bleakly, as she cupped the plastic mug between her hands. 'The pressure of the business and his other health problems. I believe he talked to you about them.' Cenna made no comment as Mary continued. 'He's seen the consultant, but we don't know how long it will be before he can have the cyst removed. Anyway, that doesn't seem important now. I just have difficulty in accepting Ray has a heart problem. He's so active and he doesn't smoke.'

'Is there a history in the family of any heart-related problems?' Cenna asked.

'I've no idea,' Mary shrugged. 'Ray was fostered as a child. Do you think it could be inherited?'

'Possibly. High blood pressure is a major risk factor as is a raised blood cholesterol level. How's Ray's diet?'

'He's a chef,' Mary shrugged. 'What can I say? And you've seen him. There's no fat on him at all. The last person I would have thought to have a heart attack.'

They sat quietly for a moment then Cenna asked, 'Have you someone to look after the hotel?'

Mary nodded slowly. 'I rang our manageress this morning when Ray began to feel unwell. And the second chef will have to cope until we find someone to replace Ray whilst he's ill.'

A door opened and the ward sister appeared. 'Mrs Gardiner, would you like to come in?'

Mary stood up. 'How is he?'

'Feeling much more comfortable and asking for you.' The sister smiled.

'Keep in touch,' Cenna said, rising to her feet and briefly touching Mary's arm before she left.

When Cenna arrived home, the phone was ringing. She hurried to answer it, hoping it was Phil, but it wasn't. Sue Compton, treasurer of the gym club, wanted to confirm the holiday arrangements.

Cenna talked for a while, telling herself what she was doing was for the best.

'Any chance of Phil coming with you?' Sue asked. 'Mike's dropped out at the last moment.'

'No,' Cenna told her. 'I'm afraid not.'

She was at the end of pretending. Almost.

A week later Homer Pomeroy arrived at the surgery, deeply tanned and full of smiles.

'How was the holiday?' Cenna asked.

'As you can see, I behaved myself.'

'You look very fit.'

He beamed her a smile and handed her a buff-coloured envelope. 'For you and Dr Jardine, my dear.'

Cenna pulled out the card. 'An engagement party?'

'Mrs Vine and I decided to tie the knot. It's rather short notice but we decided whilst on holiday. You'll both be able to come, I hope? It was you and Dr Jardine that day who knocked some sense into an old man's head.'

'I'm flattered, but it was you who made up your mind to make changes. And you've kept to them.'

'Life is very much worth living.' Homer cleared his throat. 'Can I take it we shall have the pleasure of your company?'

Cenna glanced at the dates. 'I'll talk with Dr Jardine and let you know.'

'You do that.' Homer rose. 'We shall both be very disappointed if we don't see you.'

After surgery, Cenna went into Phil's room. He had just seen his last patient and with a grin examined the invitation. 'Sounds fun. A marquee—and live music.' He glanced at the door and then came round the desk and took her in his arms. 'How do you feel about dancing the night away?'

'I'd like nothing more, but it's the night before I leave.'

He paused, his eyebrows shooting up. 'Oh.'

'Maybe we could dance half the night away.'

'I don't think I'll want to share you with anyone else.' He held her face between his hands, smoothing her cheeks with the pads of his thumbs.

'Don't let's decide now. I told Homer I would let him know. There's no rush.'

'What do you say to a take-away this evening and…an early night?'

'I'm on call.'

He sighed and pulled a face. 'When will I see you next?'

'Sunday afternoon. Jane and Marcus have asked us to tea.'

He slowly lowered his head. His kiss was long and tender. 'I suppose that will have to do for now.'

'Sunday evening's free…' she murmured breathlessly.

'No it's not,' he muttered. 'It's booked. With me.'

Jane had set tea in the garden on the table under the umbrella. Lifting the last tray of pastries and croissants from the kitchen worktop, she glanced out through the window. Her heart still beat fast when she caught sight of her husband. He was sitting beside Phil who was bouncing five-month-old Emma on his knee. The frill of the large green umbrella waved gently in the breeze. Cenna's dark head, covered by a straw Bo-Peep hat, was bent over Ben who was engrossed in a book.

Jane wished she had a camera. It would have been a perfect photo for the family album. She was, however, concerned for her friend. Cenna had seemed distant these last few days. Was it Phil? she wondered. Odd they weren't going away together—but Cenna had said nothing about the separately booked holidays.

Taking the tray out into the garden, Jane caught the last part of the conversation.

'I'm hoping I won't need to take very much,' Cenna was saying in answer to Marcus's question. 'Mostly T-shirts, shorts and swimwear.'

'Are there any sharks in the sea at Crete?' Ben asked, closing his atlas.

Marcus chuckled. 'Hope not, young man.'

Cenna's amber eyes met Jane's. 'Look what your mum has brought. Scrumptious.'

'Is this all for me?' Marcus joked. 'Where is everyone else's?'

'Uncle Phil, are you going to Crete, too?'

'No, I'm afraid not, Ben.'

'Where are you staying, Cenna?' Jane asked quickly, sensing that her son had strayed onto a sensitive issue.

'Aghios Nikolaos, a little seaside village. The club hired a yacht and we'll be able to dive and ski just off the harbour.'

'Sounds idyllic,' said Marcus, devouring a doughnut. 'I doubt if we'll be following in your footsteps for a year or two.'

'Are you going inland?' Jane continued, attempting to lighten the atmosphere.

'If time allows,' Cenna answered in a subdued voice. 'Maybe up to the Lasithi Plain which is supposed to be very beautiful.'

'It sounds wonderful. I'm envious.'

Jane glanced at Cenna. Her hair was coiled up and pinned with a fashionable comb and her light tan gave even more depth to her amber eyes. She looked cool and very lovely, but Jane knew something was wrong.

'I think we'll have to wait a while until Emma is older,' Marcus said as he downed a large cup of tea.

'Give Emma a couple more seasons and she'll be ready for her first dip.' Phil curled his long tanned fingers over Emma's small head. The baby gurgled, her lovely blue eyes twinkling under her tuft of blonde hair.

'She even eats real food now,' Ben said, fortunately changing the subject to babies. When most of the pastries and croissants had been eaten and the table cleared, the men disappeared into the house.

'Cricket's on TV,' sighed Jane, stretching out on a steamer chair. 'Ben's crazy about it.'

'He adores Emma, that's obvious,' Cenna said as she rocked Emma in her pram.

Jane rested her elbows on the table and smiled. 'You know that your suggestion at the hospital did the trick. About collecting Ben from school? It was the turning point. He must have needed reassurance that I wasn't going to be away for ever. I feel confident enough now to think about work. In fact, I've made enquiries at the local nursery. At the end of September they can take Emma twice a week.'

'So you're seriously considering returning before Christmas?'

Jane nodded. 'Part time, of course.'

'Have you talked to Marcus about it?'

Jane smiled ruefully. 'The subject came up the other evening. Did you know Helen Prior has put out feelers for a partnership?'

'Yes, I did.'

'How would you feel if Helen joined the practice?' Jane asked.

For a long while Cenna was silent, then she met Jane's eyes. 'To be honest, Jane, it won't affect me. After my holiday I'm leaving.'

'Leaving?' Jane stared at her. 'But, Cenna, why?' When she didn't answer, Jane realised the reason. 'It's Phil, isn't it?'

'Not entirely.' Cenna sighed and nodded. 'But mostly, yes.'

'It's not working out between you?'

'He's shut himself off, Jane, so completely, I don't know how to get through.'

'Does he know how you feel about him?'

'If he did it wouldn't make any difference. It's still Maggie—and always will be.'

'But Maggie's gone and she'll never come back,' Jane protested gently.

'No,' Cenna answered, her face devoid of emotion. 'Maggie never left. She's in his heart and he doesn't want to let her go.'

'And so you're giving up?'

'Jane, I don't want to let him go. But I can't compete with her any longer.'

Jane understood what Cenna was saying. She recalled the desperation she had felt at giving up Marcus, the long years without him after Katrina had died. The insecurities of their love at first, overshadowed by Katrina's ghost. But their love had won through in the end. If only Cenna would try a little longer...

'Does Phil know you're leaving?' Jane asked.

'Not yet.'

'Where will you go? Have you made any plans?'

'Abroad, I think,' Cenna answered quietly. 'I've been doing a little research. There's plenty of scope for English GPs. And I have no ties, no commitments here in England.'

'Cenna, is there nothing I can say to change your mind?' Jane asked. 'I would hate to lose you as a friend as well as a colleague. We all would. Phil will be devastated.'

Cenna's eyes came up slowly and to Jane's surprise she nodded. 'Yes, I know that. Phil himself said I make the perfect partner.' She smiled wistfully. 'And that, ironically, is the reason I'm leaving.'

CHAPTER TWELVE

ON THE first Monday in September, it was back to normal hours at the surgery. Cenna arrived at eight and Phil was in the office when she entered. He looked up, smiling at once though his dark eyes were tired and there was a slight shadow on his jaw.

'Busy night?' she guessed, knowing he had been on weekend call.

'A visit in the early hours—then again at three and another at four. Two of them were admissions, an elderly lady who had fallen and a child with abdominal pain. I didn't manage much sleep after that.'

She sat down beside him. He looked in need of a hug and his grin told her he was thinking the same thing.

'Come for a meal after work,' she said. 'I'll do something easy. An omelette and salad. Then you can escape for an early night.'

One dark eyebrow moved upward. 'The omelette sounds wonderful. I'm not so certain about escaping.'

She smiled. 'Nor me.'

'What would sound more promising,' he told her in a low voice, his eyes meeting hers, 'would be coffee and your company afterwards.'

'Hmm…coffee's easy. And the company even easier.'

'Then you're on.'

'What have you got there?' She saw the pile of post, recently opened, on the desk. He lifted the top letter and handed it to her.

'It's Barry Thornton. The guy we dug out of the blue Vauxhall.'

She glanced at the letter from Southampton Hospital where the road accident victim had been admitted. It was relatively good news and she glanced at Phil. 'He's had a metal plate put in his spine?'

Phil nodded. 'They also gave him methylprednisolone within a few hours of the injury. Whether or not it was that or the surgeon's skill in removing the pressure on the spine that helped, I don't suppose we'll ever know.'

'A combination of both perhaps,' murmured Cenna. 'He'll walk again, won't he?'

'In time, yes. Lucky man.'

'Just lucky you were there.'

Phil shrugged. 'Odd when you think about it. We wouldn't have gone that route if we hadn't been late.'

It was a sobering thought, one on which Cenna had dwelt on many times since the accident. And she knew as she met Phil's eyes that he had, too.

'Treatment will be directed now towards preventing secondary problems.' Cenna read from the letter. 'Physio to avoid joints locking and muscles contracting.'

'A long haul,' Phil sighed, 'but a darn sight better than a wheelchair.'

Just then Paula entered and, glancing at her watch, said, 'Your first patients are in. Mrs Gardiner for you, Dr Jardine, and Louise Ryman for you, Dr Lloyd.'

'Give us a couple of minutes, Annie,' Phil replied with a grin. 'Just glancing through the post.'

'Fine. Let me know when you're ready.'

'Mary Gardiner,' Phil murmured after Annie left. 'I don't usually see her. You do.'

'Perhaps it's with regard to Ray,' Cenna suggested.

'Yes. Possibly. We had a report from the hospital last week. He's up and about and they'll do a full assessment of the heart's condition through outpatient appointments.'

Then his gaze came up to meet hers. 'Is the omelette still on?'

'Coffee afterwards, too, if you want.'

'I want,' he muttered. Standing, he bent quickly to brush his lips over her mouth.

Later, in her own room, Cenna glanced through Louise Ryman's notes. The last time she had seen Louise she had prescribed antidepressants. But when Louise entered it wasn't the pale and tired-looking girl of a few weeks ago. Her long auburn hair was fashioned into a bob and she wore make-up, a suit and high heels.

'You're looking much better,' Cenna told her as Louise sat down and opened her shoulder-bag.

She brought out a small brown bottle and passed it to Cenna. 'I'm showing off, I'm afraid.'

Cenna frowned as she saw the bottle was almost full.

'I took a few,' Louise went on to tell her, 'but most of the pills are still there. I'll return them to the pharmacy but I wanted to show you first. My last visit to you, Dr Lloyd, certainly helped, but it wasn't because of the antidepressants. Though, in a way, I suppose it was fate that I cut my finger that day and came to the surgery.'

'I'm intrigued.' Cenna said, handing back the bottle.

Louise smiled. 'Whilst I was waiting to see you, I spoke to a young man whose father is a fisherman. He owns the seafish shop on the harbour.'

'Steven Oakman—Clyde Oakman's son? Yes, I saw him that morning, too.'

Louise nodded. 'We commented on our injuries and fell into conversation, only to discover our mutual interest in information technology.' To Cenna's slow smile, Louise added quickly, 'No, there's no romance, Dr Lloyd. It will be a long time before I can love someone again as much as I loved Martin. Steve and I are just good friends—or rather business partners now.'

'Business partners?' Cenna repeated, her curiosity deepening.

'Yes. I told him I was an IT teacher and he explained he'd just got his degree but hadn't managed to find work. We swapped email addresses and the outcome is we've formed an Internet agency providing specialist databases and services.'

'You've left teaching?' Cenna asked in surprise.

'Yes. Steve and I have been working hard throughout the summer to get the agency off the ground. I also sold the house last month and moved into a flat. This gave me some financial breathing space. Steve will still help his father part time but…' Louise smiled as she added, 'Mr Oakman is now a client on our database. I'm pleased to say his business is improving already with the aid of his website. So, you see, I have you to thank really for my new direction.'

'I wish—' Cenna grinned '—we could help all our patients so effectively.'

'I'll give my change of address in at the desk,' Louise said as she rose. 'Though I'm not looking forward to telling Mrs Sharpe. I taught her son, Callum, you know.'

Cenna raised her eyebrows. 'You'll be missed at school.'

And predictably, after surgery, Annie knocked and came into Cenna's room. 'You know about Louise leaving school?' she said, and Cenna nodded. 'Callum will miss her. She was a good teacher. I regret that I haven't really encouraged his IT studies enough. But with what Louise was telling me, I think we should invest in a computer for the house.'

When Annie had bustled out again, Cenna remembered that she had to visit the supermarket before going home. Even an omelette required eggs. She left slightly early that evening, relieved that there were no extra TRs to see. By the time she had done her shopping and arrived home, it was gone six. Phil would call any moment and she took a hurried shower and changed into jeans and a T-shirt.

When he arrived, Phil took her in his arms as usual, barely giving her time to speak. She never failed to be surprised at their need for one another, his mouth crushing down on hers, leaving her fighting with the urge to leave supper and tug him upstairs.

But good sense prevailed and reluctantly she broke away, leading him into the kitchen. He sat on the stool and leaned an elbow on the worktop. He drew his large, summer-tanned hands over his face, then loosened his tie, a gesture she always found too sexy to ignore.

'Busy day?' she asked, attempting to concentrate on washing the salad.

He came up behind her and slid his arms around her waist. 'Not too bad. What can I do? Shall I wash the salad for you?'

'No. Make yourself a coffee. Or there's a beer in the fridge. Or wine.'

'Cenna…' Nestling his mouth against her neck, she gave up trying to work and, turning slowly, she lifted her face. He bent his head and kissed her for a long, slow time until finally he drew away. 'That's better. That slakes the thirst.'

She smiled softly and in a soft voice whispered, 'Do you want to sit in the garden? There's still a little sun.'

'Are you trying to get rid of me?' He grinned and let her go, settling himself back on the stool. He took off his suit jacket and laid it across his knees, grinning up at her. She picked up the egg again, forcing her gaze from the broad shoulders and long, outspread legs. 'How was Mary Gardiner?' she asked, picking up the whisk and adding cheese and garlic.

'Ray's probably being discharged next week.'

'Oh. Not to start work again immediately, I hope?'

'No. They're selling up. Mary asked me to tell you.'

'Selling up?' Cenna turned to frown at him. 'Because of Ray's health?'

'Mary feels they work too hard and too long for too little. With what happened in the summer with the Marchants and facing a pretty tough winter building up trade again, they've decided to call it a day.'

'Understandable,' Cenna said quietly. 'And probably it's a sensible decision. Do they have any plans for the future?'

'Mary has friends in the south of France. Winemakers. They want partners and Mary and Ray know something about the business. It seemed, Mary said, like fate is taking them down that road.'

'Twice today, fate has been mentioned,' Cenna said ruefully. 'One of my patients told me that meeting another patient in the waiting room had changed the course of her life.'

'And this makes a third time,' Phil said in a husky growl as he cast his jacket onto the stool beside him and stood up. He walked towards her and this time he didn't hold back. Pulling her against his chest, his kisses demanded nothing less than her immediate response. She closed her eyes, her heart thumping wildly under her ribs as his tongue slipped searchingly between her teeth. His kiss left her breathless and when he finally gave her a chance to breathe he muttered, 'Fate has just decreed the omelette will have to wait because I certainly can't.'

It was as if, during Cenna's last three weeks at the surgery, Phil suspected something was wrong. Sometimes he watched her. She could never read his expression. She told herself that she was acting normally. If anything, she talked too much or made conversation to avoid pauses. Pauses that once would have been innocent. When her mind hadn't been planning ahead. When she wasn't, even at this eleventh hour, hoping for the words that would change her life.

'Tell him you love him,' Jane had urged her.

She had wanted to tell him so many times. Never more than when she would be leaving. 'Let's eat out,' Phil had suggested, momentarily swaying her resolve. 'A country inn—the New Forest, perhaps. Somewhere romantic.'

But she'd shaken her head. 'We should go to Homer's party,' she'd told him.

'I have to agree it's not every day we get the chance of a marquee and champagne,' he'd said, agreeing too easily.

Her reasons for going to Homer's engagement party were complicated. If she was alone all night with him, it would be a risk. She didn't want to weaken. She had to be strong…keep focused. If she didn't, she'd convince herself she was wrong. That she was happy the way they were. After all, didn't they have a perfect partnership?

She had gone over it a thousand times in her head.

The little flame of hope had refused to be extinguished.

Tell me you love me, she'd pleaded silently. Just three words and I'll love you for ever, make you forget Maggie.

But he hadn't told her.

And she knew he wouldn't.

It was a warm September evening, with the sun shimmering through the trees of her small garden, giving the air a silvery look. The sycamores reminded Cenna of earlier that year, when she had stood gazing out of the surgery window, watching Phil and Helen.

Helen arrived twice weekly on Tuesdays and Thursdays. She had successfully assisted with surgeries and though she was due to finish whilst Cenna was away on holiday, Phil hadn't commented on whether Helen had yet applied for a partnership.

Cenna looked down at her bed. On top of it there were three small piles of clothing to be added to her suitcase. Everything else was packed. She had spent the day in preparation for tomorrow, trying not to think about tonight. Phil was due to arrive at seven and drive them out to Homer's party. She had yet to decide what she was going to wear.

There was a floaty green summer dress, a pale blue trouser suit or a long black skirt and a top that sparkled with tiny multicoloured beads woven into the fabric. None of these, however, seemed appropriate for Homer's party and she finally she decided on a dove grey dress that was just a little too sophisticated for most occasions. The last time she'd worn it had been to a wedding of one of the girls at the gym club. Then she had teamed it with a large light grey brimmed hat and pearls, but tonight she would rely on its simple slim-fitting cut alone.

A delicate golden chain around her neck and gold studs in her ears were the only accessories she chose to wear, plus a liberal spray of her favourite perfume. Her dark, shining hair she left free, the ends turning under into a soft bob just above her shoulders. Slipping into high heels and clutching a small purse, she felt ready for the evening.

Phil arrived on the dot. He was dressed in a black dinner suit and looked stunningly handsome. His dark hair was brushed across his head smoothly and his height and breadth were perfect for the suit he wore. For once he didn't step into the house and take her into his arms. He stood instead, on the doorstep, drinking her in.

'I've never seen you in that dress before,' he said quietly.

'No. I don't wear it very often.'

'You should do.' He met her eyes and for a moment she stood where she was, inhaling him and the evening breeze as it blew in softly through the door.

Then all at once he was stepping in and closing the door with his heel. His kiss stole away any traces of the lipstick she'd attempted to apply, and when he lifted his head his eyes were filled with desire. 'Do we have to go tonight?'

he muttered as she pushed herself away gently. 'A sudden case of flu wouldn't wash?'

'I don't think so.'

'What time do you leave tomorrow?'

'Eleven.' The club had hired a small coach and they were meeting at the gym.

She gazed up into the deep brown eyes and he lifted her hair, let the silky heaviness of it fall through his fingers. Bending down, he kissed the soft, scented skin behind her ear. 'I'll miss you,' he whispered.

She looked at his head, bent against her, at the thick and beautiful pelt of hair that she loved to distraction. And she prayed silently. Say it now. Say those three words. Please, say them.

But instead he turned her slowly towards him. With a tender finger he traced the outline of her features as if committing them to memory. Then with a sigh that seemed to come from deep in his chest, he nodded slowly. 'In which case, my sweet Cinderella, I had better have you home before midnight.'

CHAPTER THIRTEEN

CENNA'S flight to Athens left Heathrow on time, and as the plane climbed into a late afternoon sky, she laid her head back and closed her eyes. Despite the bubbling presence of Sue beside her, nothing could prevent her from thinking of last night and the desperation she had felt in leaving Phil.

'I won't come in,' he'd said quietly as he'd turned the engine of the car off outside her house. It had been later than either of them had anticipated. Homer and Edith had insisted they stay until the last dance under the huge marquee at one o'clock.

'Are you sure?' she'd whispered, wanting nothing more than his presence beside her through the night.

'No, but you need some sleep.'

'I'll have some on the plane…'

'It wouldn't be fair,' he'd said gently, tipping her chin up and gazing into her eyes. 'As much as I would like it, I won't.' Then, walking her to the door, he had kissed her in the darkness. A last kiss that had broken her heart.

As Phil had driven away, Cenna had walked numbly into the house. Then, after closing the door, she had dissolved into tears. She'd sat for a long while in the darkness, reasoning with herself.

If he loved her, he would have told her.

If he'd wanted to spend time with her, he would be here now.

Finally, she couldn't think any more. Drying her eyes, she went into the bedroom and took off her dress. She would never wear it again. It would always remind her of Phil and their last night together.

Making herself a hot drink, she packed the last of her things. When she went to bed it was close to three, yet she lay awake until streamers of light crept through the curtains. Homer's party was vague in her memory. She had got through it, laughing and smiling, aware that no luxury had been spared for the guests. But the live band, the beautiful marquee spilling with flowers and a buffet that had seemed endless, as had been the champagne, had done nothing to prevent a knot of tension forming in her stomach.

Homer's party had signalled the end of her relationship with Phil. Their last and final night together. When she returned from Crete, Helen would have approached Phil for a partnership and Jane would be starting back, too. With a full quota of staff there would be no reason to delay.

By the time the plane reached Athens it was dusk. Only the runway lights and the illumination of the airport were visible from the aeroplane window. A breathtaking heat engulfed them as they walked across the tarmac, and once through customs Cenna was grateful for the group's prior planning. A vehicle stood waiting to take them to their hotel in Plaka, the pretty nineteenth-century area of Athens.

The following morning, they visited the stunning Temple of Poseidon. After a final excursion through the little Turkish bazaars it was time to set sail for their destination, the historic port of Aghios Nikolaos. When at last they arrived, tired, hungry and thirsty, Yanni, their host, and her English husband, Peter, were there to welcome them to the hotel.

Yanni's moussaka, sargos and skorpidi fish dishes filled each of the nine hungry stomachs, and in the company of her friends Cenna forgot about home for a while as they ate alfresco. Seated either side of a long wooden table, the topic of conversation was tomorrow's itinerary of sailing, waterskiing and sea-kayaking.

But once alone in her room, Cenna's thoughts returned to England. She stood on the balcony and gazed out onto the magical scene. The harbour and its translucent blue water was hidden in darkness. Only a few lights twinkled from the boats. Pushing the balcony shutters wide open, the sounds of laughter and music drifted up from the courtyard below.

Everyone was talking and laughing. The night was filled with exotic scents and the sky above was studded with tiny, twinkling diamonds. Cenna sat on the balcony seat, gazing up at them. She wondered what Phil was doing and where he was. The hardest decision she had ever had to make had been the one to leave him.

The weather was perfect throughout the week. A cool breeze eased the effects of the glare of the sun, and on Sunday morning Cenna covered herself with a last coat of sunscreen, her tawny skin now golden and glossy. The tour bus was leaving early for the Lasithi Plateau, a beauty spot set in the heart of the Dhkiti mountains, and she arrived early for breakfast, then made a dash to the bus. The sky was slightly overcast as she boarded and a stuffy heat caused the bus driver to open the windows and complain loudly in Greek.

Cenna sat at the rear, beside the window, listening to the assortment of foreign tongues. But her attempts to distract herself soon failed and it was Phil's face and smile that came to mind. She recalled the little things—the twist of his lips before he broke into laughter, the sparkling brown of his eyes. The even rhythm of his voice, the throaty chuckle that reverberated through his chest. The thickness of his dark hair and the way he tilted his head to one side when trying to concentrate...

The ache inside her grew as she gazed through the window. Even the small hope had faded now that he might telephone the hotel. And what would she have said anyway, if he had? she asked herself.

No, it was over.

There was no going back.

The bus rumbled through the narrow streets where the tavernas were still closed, but the small, picturesque houses had their shutters thrown open to the sun. People leaned out, taking in the beautiful morning. The pace of life was slow and easy. A few cars passed, squeezing through the narrow lanes.

On the outskirts of the town the bus slowed down. A white car paused to allow it to turn across the road. Cenna could see the driver. His gaze was distracted for a moment, then all at once he was staring up at her.

Cenna sat up in her seat. She stared out of the window, her heart crashing against her ribs. Then she was rapping on the window-pane, calling out, and everyone in the bus had turned to stare at her.

As the bus groaned its way up the hill, the car was lost to sight. Cenna jumped to her feet, dragging her backpack with her. She stumbled down the aisle and arrived breathlessly by the driver.

'Stop, please, stop,' she shouted. The driver looked at her as though she were crazy. But she yelled at him again and he must have understood her.

The bus ground to a halt. Grudgingly, he allowed her to dismount. Had she imagined what she'd seen? she asked herself as she gulped in air, straining her eyes after the car. Could it have been him? Or was she a mad, crazy fool, who was so much in love she was having delusions?

Then, at the bottom of the hill, she saw a figure shimmering in the heat haze. A tall, dark-haired man wearing a white T-shirt and dark shorts was striding towards her.

Then she began running again, running as fast as she could, down the hot sandy slope and into Phil's arms.

He swept her up and swung her around. He was laughing, a deep, rich sound that came from deep down in his chest. His arms were hugging her tightly and when finally her sandalled feet touched the ground she looked up into his eyes, unable to speak. He took her face between his hands and to the curious stare of the passing traffic, crushed her against him and kissed her long and hard.

The kiss seemed to go on for ever. Cenna held onto him tightly, terrified he might disappear, but when he lifted his mouth and gazed into her eyes, she knew he was real. She could taste him, see him, feel him and smell him, a man whom she'd imagined to be thousands of miles away in England.

'Surprised?' he whispered huskily.

All she could do was nod. She didn't trust herself to speak.

He took hold of her hand. 'Come on, the car's at the bottom of the hill.'

The white car was parked unceremoniously on the side of the road. He opened the door and she slid in.

'I'll warn you now,' he told her as he sat beside her, his dark eyes determined, 'I have no intention of letting you out of my sight for the next twenty-four hours at least. If you have any objection to that, then you had better—'

He broke off as she began to laugh, tears of joy running down her cheeks. He wiped them away with the pads of his thumbs and began laughing, too, until finally, taking her in his arms, he silenced her with a long and breathless kiss.

Phil tenderly laid her on the bed, lowering his lips to hers. As passion overtook them, for the first time in weeks Cenna felt the ache inside her diminish. He made love to her with infinite tenderness and when it was over he cradled her against him, whispering words she'd thought she would never hear.

To the sounds of the tiny hotel going about its business, Cenna lay fulfilled and at peace in his arms. He turned her gently towards him, his dark eyes roving over her sun-tanned arms and the soft swell of her breasts under the white cover. His fingers played in her hair, softly caressing her scalp as she drank in the sight of his dark, grainy skin and beautiful brown eyes.

'I missed you,' he told her with a shuddering sigh. 'More than I ever imagined possible. I've been such a fool.'

She lifted her face and gazed into his eyes. 'You came all this way, Phil. But why?'

'Isn't that obvious? I couldn't stand another day without you.'

'You could have phoned…'

'I wanted to look into your eyes,' he muttered as he propped himself up on one arm, 'when I told you there was no way I was going to accept your resignation.'

'My resignation?' She sat up slowly. 'But how did you know?'

'A mutual friend told me. And thank God she did.'

'You mean Jane?'

'I was so damn miserable, I left her no choice. Cenna, why didn't you tell me you were planning to leave?'

She looked down at his large strong hands covering hers so tenderly. 'I don't know where to begin…'

'The beginning will do fine,' he told her softly. 'We'll take it from there.'

She sighed, meeting his gaze. She had to tell him the truth now. 'I can't settle for half of you, Phil. Maggie will always be between us. I can't fight her. I tried, but she's too strong.'

He gripped her fingers and she looked up. 'Yes, she *was*

always there, I can't deny that, my darling. But not now. I want that to change. I want you—I want us.'

Cenna looked anxiously into his face. 'I'd like to believe that, Phil.'

'You have to,' he said urgently. 'You must. Meeting Maggie wasn't real. It was like a dream, a fantasy, with both of us playing parts. Maggie was infatuated with a man she thought could cure her and I was flattered—and amazed—by her attention. It's so easy to fool oneself when you think you want something.'

Cenna thought how that could have applied to herself and Mark all those years ago. Even though a friend had told her that Mark had been seeing someone else, she had at first refused to believe the truth.

'After we were married,' Phil continued urgently, 'Maggie told me about the anorexia and I agreed to treat her. She begged me to tell no one. Her career was at stake, she said, and I knew what it meant to her so I agreed. The only people we could talk to were Gwen and Derek but it was too late for them to help. They had known for a long time that Maggie was out of control. In the end I realised that, too. I failed her, Cenna. I couldn't give her what she wanted.'

'That's not true, Phil,' Cenna protested. 'I know you. You wouldn't have given up. You're a good doctor, a capable one. Maggie couldn't really have wanted to be cured.'

'I'll never know,' he told her hollowly. 'You see, I gave her an ultimatum. I knew it was either specialist help or we wouldn't survive. I told her I wasn't prepared to go on hiding the anorexia, that she had to seek treatment. I expected a flat refusal. Instead, she told me she needed time to think—a holiday. The rest you know.'

'But that wasn't your fault. You can't blame yourself for an accident. We were involved in an accident ourselves, remember? A few seconds later and perhaps neither of us would be here now. It was no one's fault. It just happened that way. Maggie wasn't killed because of your ultimatum. She was killed because of the avalanche.'

He sighed, shaking his head. 'You don't understand…'

Cenna looked at him, her heart aching for him. 'Then make me understand, Phil. Tell me…'

He swallowed, his eyes coming up to meet hers. 'I've always feared that she was so confused…that she…tried to kill herself.' His voice caught in his throat and pain filled his eyes. 'Which is why I felt so responsible…and why I had to see Gwen…to try and resolve my feelings of guilt.'

'But, Phil,' Cenna pleaded gently, 'Maggie died in an accident. You weren't to blame and mustn't lose sight of that. Gwen knew how hard you tried to help her daughter—you did everything humanly possible.'

'I tried,' he muttered grimly, 'but did I try hard enough? If I had sought help, maybe she would be alive today.'

Cenna shook her head slowly. 'Maggie didn't want help. What would you have done if, after the holiday, she'd still refused treatment? Would you have left her?'

He paused, his brown eyes lowered in thought. 'No. But I think Maggie would have left me.'

'Then you've nothing to reproach yourself for. You kept Maggie's secret—none of us ever guessed at the truth. It was what Maggie wanted. You didn't give up on her. You tried your best.'

He reached out and brought her closer, brushing his cheek against her hair. 'I felt I didn't have the right to love you,' he whispered hoarsely. 'I'd made such a mess of things before.'

She reached up to slide her arms around his neck. 'Everyone deserves a second chance, Phil. Don't we?'

'Oh, God, Cenna. What an idiot I've been.'

She smiled tentatively. 'Make love to me again.'

He slid down beside her, pulling her into his arms, and the words he murmured were all that she had ever wanted to hear.

EPILOGUE

CENNA slowly turned the pages of the album. Her intention was to avoid the amused stare of her husband sitting in the chair opposite her. But as his strong, tanned fingers drummed on the desk, she was forced to look up.

'It was an easy mistake to make,' she murmured—pathetically. 'Helen said that you'd mentioned Jane might not be returning—'

'Temporarily,' Phil corrected her, one eyebrow shooting up.

'But Helen didn't say that—'

'Because you didn't ask.'

'All right. Because I didn't ask. And because I assumed—'

'That the albums she was talking about were ones I kept at home. Which I didn't. Dozens of loose photos stacked away in some shoebox probably, yes. But no albums. Not until I met and married my most recent wife.'

Cenna glared at him, almost throwing the surgery album at him but deciding not to. It was full of lovingly pasted souvenirs, newspaper cuttings, letters and photos of the opening of Nair Surgery three years ago.

She closed it carefully. 'You can't deny,' she went on, unwilling to allow Phil the last word on the subject, 'that Helen did fancy a partnership with you. And not entirely a professional one.'

Phil rose, holding up the palms of his hands in submission. 'I repeat, the only time I have ever discussed a partnership—''a perfect partnership''—was with a certain member of the practice who shall be nameless. Now, come here, wife, and stop nagging me.'

Cenna glanced at her husband and grinned. Crete seemed a long time ago now—a year almost to the day. However, they were soon to set foot on the island again. In just a few hours their plane would be leaving London and for three wonderful weeks they would be in paradise.

'I'm not the only one who jumped to conclusions,' Cenna remarked as he reached up to remove a tiny heart of pink confetti from her dark hair. 'You actually believed Mark when he told you we were an item!'

Phil rolled his eyes. 'You forget, he was standing on your doorstep—and he did seem to appear every so often. And there was that romantic dinner at the Summerville—'

'Which you assumed was a romantic dinner,' she reminded him archly, kissing the tip of his nose.

'Touché,' Phil conceded half-heartedly. 'Though I'm not entirely convinced, Mrs Jardine, that I—apparently—had your heart in the palm of my hand.'

'What will it take to convince you?' she asked innocently, lifting her large amber eyes to his.

'A small hotel on a Mediterranean island,' he growled into her neck, 'a bottle of champagne and a room with a large double bed.'

'I liked the last room.'

'This time we have the honeymoon suite,' he muttered, kissing her firmly. Taking her wrist, he propelled her towards the door.

'Don't tell me you know the Greek for honeymoon suite!'

'No, but I made myself plain enough. Yanni understood quite clearly. Now, if you've finished hauling me down memory lane, it's time we left.'

Cenna glanced one last time around her room. She didn't regret persuading Phil into the unscheduled visit to the surgery before leaving for their honeymoon. After all, a gorgeous digital photograph taken by Marcus of their wedding had to be pasted into the last page of the office album. It seemed the perfect offering of thanks to the hand of fate that had finally brought them true happiness.

She was suddenly swept off her feet and up into Phil's strong arms. 'It looks as though I'm going to have to be firm with my new wife,' Phil scolded her as she let out a squeal.

'Promises, promises,' she whispered, curling her arms around his neck.

He grinned down at her and nodded. 'And this is one I definitely intend to keep.'

Modern Romance™
...seduction and
passion guaranteed

Tender Romance™
...love affairs that
last a lifetime

Sensual Romance™
...sassy, sexy and
seductive

Blaze™
...sultry days and
steamy nights

Medical Romance™
...medical drama on
the pulse

Historical Romance™
...rich, vivid and
passionate

29 new titles every month.

*With all kinds of Romance for
every kind of mood...*

MILLS & BOON®

Makes any time special™

MAT4

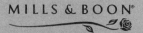

MILLS & BOON®

Medical Romance™

EMERGENCY WEDDING by *Marion Lennox*

When Dr Susie Ellis returns to the surgery she part-owns in Whale Beach, Australia, she finds the handsome Dr Darcy Hayden in residence. She needs to work to support her coming baby and he can't leave because of his young son, but only one doctor can stay at the small practice. Unless they get married…

A NURSE'S PATIENCE by *Jessica Matthews*

Part 2 of Nurses Who Dare

Experience had taught Dr Ryan Gregory to be wary of his colleagues, and his outgoing nurse practitioner, Amy Wyman, was furious that he wanted to monitor her work. Her fiery nature was making him nervous professionally—and passionate in private. Unless Amy learnt some patience and Ryan started to trust, their lives were going to implode.

ENGAGING DR DRISCOLL by *Barbara Hart*

Petra must resist her feelings for the gorgeous new doctor at her practice, as he is obviously involved with someone else, and Petra is engaged! Adam has other ideas, believing that Petra deserves someone better than her fiancé—like himself?

On sale 2nd November 2001

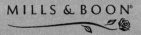

Medical Romance™

FATHER IN SECRET by *Fiona McArthur*

Dr Theo McWilliam's life was complicated enough before Sister Savannah Laine arrived, and now their growing attraction was making it difficult for him to tell her about his young son. But Savannah had already been hurt by another man's secrets, and Theo had to find a way to reveal his without losing her!

DR CARLISLE'S CHILD by *Carol Marinelli*

Working alongside each other in the busy paediatric unit of Melbourne Central was too much temptation for single father Dr Seb Carlisle and consultant Lucinda Chambers. Six weeks after the inevitable happened, she began to suspect that Seb was going to be a father again. Now she just had to figure out a way to tell him!

MIDWIFE AND MOTHER by *Lilian Darcy*

Obstetrician Alec Rostrevor knows that Erin is heartbroken when their wedding is cancelled due to the sudden illness of his baby son and reappearance of his ex-wife. He also knows that he moved twelve thousand miles to be with the woman he loves, and he has no intention of losing her now…

On sale 2nd November 2001

1001/03b

MILLS & BOON®

Christmas
with a Latin Lover

Three brand-new stories

Lynne Graham
Penny Jordan
Lucy Gordon

Published 19th October

The perfect gift this Christmas from

4 FREE
books and a surprise gift!

We would like to take this opportunity to thank you for reading this Mills & Boon® book by offering you the chance to take FOUR more specially selected titles from the Medical Romance™ series absolutely FREE! We're also making this offer to introduce you to the benefits of the Reader Service™—

- ★ FREE home delivery
- ★ FREE gifts and competitions
- ★ FREE monthly Newsletter
- ★ Exclusive Reader Service discounts
- ★ Books available before they're in the shops

Accepting these FREE books and gift places you under no obligation to buy, you may cancel at any time, even after receiving your free shipment. Simply complete your details below and return the entire page to the address below. *You don't even need a stamp!*

YES! Please send me 4 free Medical Romance books and a surprise gift. I understand that unless you hear from me, I will receive 6 superb new titles every month for just £2.49 each, postage and packing free. I am under no obligation to purchase any books and may cancel my subscription at any time. The free books and gift will be mine to keep in any case.

M1ZEA

Ms/Mrs/Miss/Mr ....Initials................................
BLOCK CAPITALS PLEASE
Surname ....
Address ....

....

....Postcode.................................

Send this whole page to:
UK: FREEPOST CN81, Croydon, CR9 3WZ
EIRE: PO Box 4546, Kilcock, County Kildare (stamp required)